Love is
a time of enchantment:
in it all days are fair and all fields
green. Youth is blest by it,
old age made benign:
the eyes of love see
roses blooming in December,
and sunshine through rain. Verily
is the time of true-love
a time of enchantment — and
Oh! how eager is woman
to be bewitched!

LET YOUR HEART ANSWER

Grace West had always obeyed her rich father's wishes — to the point of accepting Dick Browning's marriage proposal. Then union organizer Geoff Bailey came to Branton, a man as brash as Dick was cool, a man who challenged the rule of Mr. West himself. Whom did Grace truly love? It would become a tragic question that only time and her heart could answer . . .

CLARISSA ROSS

◆

LET YOUR HEART ANSWER

Complete and Unabridged

ULVERSCROFT
Leicester

First published in the
United States of America

First Large Print Edition
published December 1994

British Library CIP Data

Ross, W. E. D.
   Let your heart answer.—Large print ed.—
Ulverscroft large print series: romance
I. Title
823.914 [F]

ISBN 0–7089–3210–X

Published by
F. A. Thorpe (Publishing) Ltd.
Anstey, Leicestershire
Set by Words & Graphics Ltd.
Anstey, Leicestershire
Printed and bound in Great Britain by
T. J. Press (Padstow) Ltd., Padstow, Cornwall

This book is printed on acid-free paper

1

IT was a sunny June morning, and Grace West had just finished playing her usual early game of golf with the Branton Country Club pro. She had entered the imposing clubhouse to make a phone call to her Aunt Florence with whom she planned to have lunch.

She made her way across the deserted main lounge with its high ceiling, huge stone fireplace at one end, and glassed-in veranda overlooking the course at the other. Arranged on the mantel above the fireplace was a row of shining silver trophy cups. It gave her a moment of inner satisfaction to know that she had been responsible for winning several of them.

Grace was twenty-three and had finished college exactly a year ago. She'd trained as a lab technician and planned to take a position in the hospital in Portland or perhaps go even as far afield as Boston. She knew her father wouldn't hear of her going anywhere she couldn't come back from on weekends. Since her mother's death a decade ago he'd been inordinately possessive of her and Marie, her nineteen-year-old sister. Marie had taken the situation in her own hands and solved it in her stubborn fashion by running off to New York as soon as Grace had graduated. This had left Grace in an unhappy position. Her father had come to depend on her more than ever, and knowing how upset he was about Marie, she'd hesitated to make any move.

Finding the coin, she lifted the receiver of the pay phone and prepared to make her call. She had auburn hair of almost shoulder length slicked back from her attractive oval face with a wide black band. Her eyes were green and large with an intelligent luminosity. She had the high-coloring of an outdoor type toned by a fashionable tan and a lithe, medium-sized, athletic body.

As she waited, the phone at the other end of the line rang several times.

A precise, elderly voice answered "Yes?" The question was phrased querulously.

"It's Grace West," she said, recognizing the voice of her aunt's housekeeper, Mamie Dever. "Is Aunt Florence up yet?"

"Just," the old woman said. "Hold on a minute. I'll try and get her to take the call in her bedroom."

"Thanks," Grace said with resignation, a faint smile crossing her face with its good high-cheeked bone structure and the scattering of tiny freckles under her tan.

After a moment there was a crackling sound at the other end and Aunt Florence spoke in her fretful, nervous manner, "Is that you, Grace?"

"Yes, Aunt Flo," she said dutifully. "I wondered about lunch. Are you planning to drive over to the club or would you rather I come to your place?"

"Where are you now?"

"At the clubhouse. I've just finished a game with Jamie. I'm going to do some practice shots for the rest of the morning. I'll wait here if you're coming."

"I don't think so," her aunt said uncertainly. "I had a terrible night last night. My insomnia is worse than ever.

3

I kept thinking of Marie. She is coming home, isn't she?"

Grace restrained an annoyed sigh and, instead told the older woman, "Yes. She is."

"When?"

"Some time this week. That's what her letter said."

"She's always so vague," Aunt Florence fretted. "I can't imagine where she gets it from."

This coming from Aunt Florence who was vagueness personified was amusing enough to restore Grace's smile and good humor. She pointed out, "We haven't decided about lunch yet."

"Come to my place," Aunt Florence said. "I'll be no more than dressed by the time you get here."

"Very well," Grace said. "What time will that be?"

"Make it twelve-thirty," her aunt said. "I suspect you'll be famished before that. I forget you rise at ridiculous hours and work up an appetite with your golf."

She laughed lightly. "I'm going to have a snack now. Coffee and toast to hold me over."

4

"Do that," her aunt said. "I don't want to worry about your being hungry in addition to everything else. How is your father?"

"I didn't see him this morning," Grace said. "But he seemed very well last night."

"Marie has given him far too much worry," Aunt Florence said with the devotion for Adam West of a spinster, older sister.

"I'll see you at twelve-thirty, then," she said, anxious to end the phone conversation.

She had hoped Aunt Florence might decide to cancel the luncheon date. But no such luck! And she knew it would be difficult. Aunt Florence, like her father, had the knack of probing for information while carrying on a seemingly innocent discussion. And she had the feeling that the older woman suspected there was something about Marie's sudden decision to come home she didn't know about. And which she intended to find out.

The truth was that Aunt Florence was rightly suspicious. Grace hadn't confided all the news in her; she'd not even told her father all that was in Marie's letter. And she had no intention of giving the facts to her aunt until she'd told her parent. This meant the luncheon could be a trying affair for Grace since Marie had written her that she was going to be married. Married to one of the hippie crowd she'd been living with in New York's Greenwich Village. And she was bringing her husband-to-be home to meet them all.

Grace sighed as she considered the reaction that might be expected from her father. Adam West was, at fifty-seven, an austere, conservative man who looked and behaved older than his years. His patrician cast of features and iron-gray hair gave him the proper air of the small town czar he was. Along with his sister, Florence, he had inherited the family fish-packing business which was Branton's chief industry. He had served several terms as mayor and was still the town's head.

He had definite ideas about running the town and his business. And the ideas struck Grace as following rather narrow lines. But both Branton and the business

6

had prospered, so she decided he must know what he was about. The same harsh rules applied to their family life, so it was no wonder Marie had eventually rebelled.

There was bound to be dynamite in Marie's return, but Grace had no idea of allowing Aunt Florence to fret, predict, and gloat over it prematurely. With that decided, she left to go to the snack bar.

It was a bright little room. An oval food bar was in the center, surrounded by stools, and it also had a few tables for four set out along the wall with windows. As she went into the snack bar, she saw Mabel Fisher, a close friend of hers, with a handsome young stranger seated at one of the tables.

Mabel, a petite dark girl, smiled and called out to her. "Hi, Grace! Come and join us!"

She hesitated and smiled. "I'm just having coffee."

"So are we," Mabel said. "And I want you to meet my cousin Geoff."

Geoff was on his feet by this time. He was a tall young man, at least six feet, she thought. His bronzed, handsome face was notable for a square determined jaw and keen gray eyes under heavy brows. The keen gray eyes were fixed on her now.

"This is Grace West," Mabel introduced her. "My cousin, Geoff Bailey."

His eyes almost made her uncomfortable, they were so carefully appraising her. "I've heard a lot about you, Miss West," he said in a pleasant manly voice.

She laughed. "I'm afraid I'm not all that notable."

"Modest!" Mabel protested. "I've shown him all the cups you've won for us."

"You must be a remarkably good golfer," he said.

"I've had remarkably good luck." And turning to the girl at the counter, she told her, "Coffee with cream, please. I'll have it at this table." Then she sat down with them.

Geoff Bailey had the chair opposite her, and his gray eyes continued to study her with undiminished interest. "You have a very swank clubhouse," he said. "I'm impressed."

Mabel gave her cousin a teasing glance. "Just because Branton has fewer than five

8

thousand people and we're isolated on the Maine coast doesn't mean we don't know how to do things well."

"I know some places that could profit by your example," he said.

Grace now studied him. "Are you holidaying in Branton?"

"Not exactly," he said. "But I'm trying to combine a holiday with my visit."

Mabel grimaced. "Another of your dedicated businessmen," she said. "Why don't you relax and enjoy yourself?" she asked him.

"I'm really doing very well," he said. "What about you, Miss West? Do you have an occupation other than golf?"

Grace thought she caught a faint note of sarcasm in his tone, and it made her angry. This along with the way he'd been staring at her made her begin to wonder about him. As a cousin of Mabel Bailey's, he didn't seem to fit. He wasn't the right type. Mabel was a daughter of one of the wealthy lumber families who did little now but live on their money. The serious Geoff didn't appear to be cast in that mold.

Rather coolly she said, "I graduated as

a lab technician. But I haven't worked at it. I've been taking care of my father."

"Oh? Your father is ill, then."

Her feeling of anger and frustration increased. "No, he is not ill," she said firmly. "But we have a large house and my mother is dead. I'm running it for him."

"Of course," he said in that slightly mocking tone.

Mabel broke in with, "Grace has made a regular martyr of herself! She's given all this past year to Adam. And I don't think he appreciates it half enough."

Geoff looked at Grace and said, "Of course, you have managed some golf."

"Yes, I have," she said.

"And she's gotten herself engaged," Mabel said with a pleased look Grace's way. "She's going to marry a local boy. The manager of her father's factory."

"Well, well!" Geoff said, as if he might have guessed this all along.

If it hadn't been for the coffee being suddenly served, Grace would have gotten up and excused herself. She had the conviction Geoff Bailey was poking fun at her.

Desperately she forced a smile and said, "I know Mr. Bailey isn't interested in all my history, Mabel."

"He'll be staying here a while," the dark girl said. "And I want him to get to know people."

"That's right," he said. "I'm anxious to meet everyone." And with a sly look her way again, "So it's not likely you'll be ever leaving Branton to work. You're going to marry and settle down right here."

"Her father is pleased," Mabel went on artlessly to Grace's extreme discomfiture. "He says that Branton is good enough for anyone. Who would want to live in one of the big cities with all the social unrest and polluted air!"

"Sounds like a convincing argument," Geoff told his cousin easily.

"Of course, you do have to go to the cities occasionally to get decent clothes and that sort of thing," Mabel said. "But I agree with Mr. West. Branton is a nice place to live."

Geoff gave her a humorous glance once again. "I'm certain you are of the same opinion, Miss West," he said.

11

"Minds aren't all that easy to read," she said.

"You mean you have other ideas?" he asked.

"I mean I don't think they'd interest you," she said firmly. And she sipped her coffee, then asked, "What are you doing here?"

He looked a trifle taken back by her direct question. Then he said, "Well, I wanted to visit Mabel and her parents. It's been a long time since I've had contact with this branch of the family. And I thought I'd take a look around."

"But you said you weren't here for pleasure alone," Grace reminded him.

"I did?" He seemed not to remember.

"I'm certain of it," she said.

Mabel nodded. "She's right, Geoff. You did tell us that."

He hesitated. "Well, I'm going to study business conditions in the area," he said. "I hope to pick up a few pointers."

"Are you going into business for yourself?" Grace asked.

"No," he said. "I once worked with the family firm. But it's gone out of existence."

It seemed Geoff wasn't going to offer much information about himself. And Grace found it hard to judge him. He had a crisp, aggressive air, but he maintained he wasn't associated with business in any way. Perhaps he was some type of professional, a doctor or even a dentist.

"Then you plan to be here awhile?" Grace said.

"I do," he said.

Mabel smiled at her across the table. "We wanted him to stay with us. After all, there are only the three of us in all that big house. But he wouldn't hear of it. He's at the Harbor Motel."

His eyes held that humorous gleam again. "I think Mabel would soon get tired of the novelty of a guest. I'd rather be on my own. Then I can remain as long as I like."

"But we are going to entertain you," Mabel insisted as she eyed her cousin fondly. "That's why I brought you here this morning to see the club and introduce you around. You can come and use the greens anytime as our guest."

"Do you play often, Mr. Bailey?" Grace asked.

13

"Don't be so formal!" Mabel protested. "His name is Geoff! Goodness!" She added the last word disgustedly.

Geoff smiled. "She's right, you know. I used to play a great deal, Grace. But just lately I've been busy."

"We must have a game one day," she said.

"I'd enjoy that," he told her.

"Be sure Dick doesn't hear about it," Mabel said. And as an explanation to Geoff, "Dick Browning is Grace's boyfriend. And he's the jealous type."

"He should be!" was Geoff's gallant comment.

Grace was feeling increasingly uneasy. It struck her that the meeting had been awkward and Mabel had said all the wrong things in the worst way. She wasn't even certain that she liked the tall Geoff, although it was hard to judge fairly under the circumstances.

Having finished her coffee she rose from the table. "I have some practice work to do before I meet Aunt Flo," she told Mabel, and with a smile for Geoff she added, "I hope you come to appreciate Branton."

"You're helping me do that already," he assured her, on his feet again.

"We'll see you at the dance tomorrow night," Mabel promised as Grace left them.

She walked swiftly out of the snack bar, not easing her pace until she was safe from their view. The conversation had left her in a strangely unsettled frame of mind. Mabel had never been too smart, and it was clear she didn't sense that her city cousin was having a quiet laugh at them and their hidebound way of life.

Grace knew she was sensitive on this score. Since coming back to live with her father and getting engaged to Dick Browning, who was a crew-cut, younger edition of Adam West, she'd tried hard to march in step with local ideas. But she hadn't by any means been always successful. Her exposure in college had given her a new slant on things, and the comfortable views of Branton were hard to embrace again.

Being the daughter of the wealthiest man in a small town had its drawbacks. Grace was expected to live up to all the traditions of a ruling family and she was forever under the scrutiny of the public eye. Whatever she or any of the others in her family did was news in Branton. 'Gossip' would be closer to it. So Marie's escapades were particularly unfortunate and difficult for her father to bear.

From Grace's standpoint they could all lead more balanced and worthwhile lives if they could escape from Branton. And yet she'd allowed herself to fall in love with Dick and so made it almost impossible for her to ever leave the small town. Dick was not going to give up his job as her father's manager, nor could she even ask him to. She'd allowed herself to be trapped. It wasn't an especially romantic way to consider an engagement but that was what linking herself with Dick meant.

She went out to the practice course and chose a club from the bag she'd left out there. Then carefully placing a ball, she took a hard swing at it and missed!

"Aye! I had the notion you'd do that!" Jamie, the withered little Scots pro said as he came up to stand by her.

"That was temper," she said.

"Aye, I ken that as well," Jamie said dourly. "I saw you when you came out of the club. You were in a high dudgeon!" His thin, mournful face under his cap showed resignation. He wore a drooping gray sweater and baggy tweed pants to give him a general appearance of untidiness. No one would have taken him for the talented instructor he was. Grace gave all credit to Jamie for the success she'd won in tournaments.

"It won't happen again," she promised.

"A woman's entitled to her rages," Jamie counseled. "But not when she has a club in her hand."

"I'll remember that."

"If it was your sister, Marie, I'd no be surprised," Jamie went on.

"I have my moments," she confessed. "You just haven't seen me at my worst. I'll work hard now. And forget all about my troubles."

Jamie nodded. "It will be better for your game."

So she resolutely put the meeting in the snack bar out of her mind as she went on practicing shots under the hot sun of the June mid-day. The club and grounds were on a hill overlooking the river. But the river was a distance away, and on hot days such as this there was little breeze from it.

By the time twelve-fifteen had arrived and she was due to leave to keep her luncheon date with Aunt Flo, it was beginning to get really warm. Her aunt's place was also on the river but several miles nearer the city. As she drove along the busy main highway, her thoughts drifted back to her meeting with Geoff Bailey. She wondered why he had made such an impression on her. Men had stared at her before without her becoming so upset. Perhaps it was because he'd been so caustic about Branton and she was touchy on the subject of the town.

He'd somehow managed to make her feel like a small-town snob, and that was the last thing she wanted to be. She could realize that he might come to this hasty conclusion about her since on the surface she was the type. Her not working and her living at home with her wealthy parent. And filling her time with golf tournaments and becoming engaged to the manager of her fathers' business. It was all true to type. But he hadn't tried to probe beneath the surface to discover what sort of person she really was before going ahead with Geoff's snide remarks.

Or had he? Had he really tried to learn something about her by provoking her into taking a stand? And had she made it more difficult for him by retreating behind an angry mask? She couldn't be sure. All she knew was that dumb Mabel Bailey had an extremely upsetting male cousin!

She wheeled her white convertible into Aunt Florence's driveway with the same angry abandon with which she'd aimed at and missed the ball. As she braked the car to a screeching halt in the gravel beside the vine-covered majestic white house, she realized she had to stop thinking about Geoff Bailey at once.

And she did. She had put him completely out of her mind by a grim exercise of will as she presented herself at the front door. It opened, and a startled looking Mamie gazed out at her.

"Something wrong with our brakes, Miss Grace?" the dumpy white-haired woman wanted to know.

19

"No," Grace said sternly. "I just came in a little too quickly."

Mamie held the door open for her. "Hope none of the cats were sunning out there," she worried.

"I didn't see them," Grace reassured her. "Where's Aunt Flo?"

"Out back on the veranda. The table's set," the old woman said.

Grace knew the house well. She had often come to play there as a little girl. Its shadowed hallways and big old-fashioned rooms with their over-supply of stuffy Victorian furniture were as familiar to her as her own home. She had grown to love the odor of stale lilac and spices and always recalled the ancient house through its pleasantly pungent odor.

Emerging into the sunlight of the ample back veranda, she discovered her Aunt Florence seated at the table. It was set for two with gleaming china and silver and a fresh white cloth. A tribute to Mamie's dedication. Aunt Florence leaned forward for her cheek to be kissed.

"You didn't have to hurry so, my dear," was her greeting. "You must have driven like the wind."

Grace touched her lips to her aunt's dry flesh. "I'm sorry," she apologized. "I turned in too abruptly. I'm certain Mamie thinks I killed her cats."

"Wouldn't mind if you had," Aunt Florence said vehemently. She was a tall, frail woman with aquiline nose, pinched face and blue-gray hair in an upsweep style. "Now do sit down and tell me all about Marie while we have our lunch."

"There isn't much to tell," Grace said warily as she sat across the table from her aunt. She gazed out toward the river as a means of diversion. "How calm the water is today."

"A good deal calmer than I am, I'm afraid," was Aunt Flo's fretful reply. "I bleed for your dear father. I really do."

"I think Dad can stand up to whatever happens," Grace said. "He hasn't been too bad about Marie living in the city." She could have added that he'd been upset only when prodded by his sister. But she skipped that.

"You call what she's been doing living?" Aunt Flo demanded in her reedy voice. "Surely you must read the newspapers. You have seen what they say

21

about those hippie places and the kind of people who infest them. Infest them is the only way to describe such conduct. To think of a West living that way!"

"I'm sure Marie can take care of herself," Grace said as Mamie came in with glasses of tomato juice which she placed before them.

"A girl of nineteen!" Aunt Flo said scornfully.

"She's much more mature than you think," Grace said.

"Not Marie!" Aunt Florence said. "She's done all the wrong things. She's not followed your example. Branton wasn't good enough for her. Nor the Branton young men! She couldn't be like you and find herself someone serious and dependable like Dick Browning. You have done well!"

Grace made no reply to this. But she experienced another of those irritating moments of doubt which had been plaguing her too often lately. And again, in spite of all the self-control she could summon, the face of that annoying Geoff Bailey came clearly to her.

2

AS lunch progressed, Aunt Florence rambled on in her vague fashion. She had given up plans for a visit to Europe in August and instead was having some friends come to stay with her. She had been asked to make an appearance at the Summer Arts Festival and be one of the judges.

"There will be entries from all New England," she explained over her coffee. "The local committee feels it stimulates interests in Branton and brings a good many extra summer tourists here."

"I hope it does," Grace said absently.

The old woman gave her a sharp look. "It seems to me you might take an interest in something else besides golf," she snapped.

"But I do!" Grace protested.

"You don't show any signs of it, Aunt Flo went on irritably. "All the time I've been talking about the Summer Arts Festival you've hardly listened."

"I'm sorry. I didn't mean to let my mind wander."

"What is wrong with you today?" her aunt wanted to know.

Grace mustered a weary smile. "I expect I'm worried about Marie and how Dad will react to her coming home." It was a subterfuge, but it would have been impossible to convey her real thoughts to the old woman.

"And well you might be," Aunt Flo sputtered, off on the subject of the errant Marie once more. "I do hope she'll behave when she returns."

"Marie isn't all that bad," she said. "It's just that she's a kind of rebel. She sees things differently from most of the people around here."

"She has a twisted viewpoint about everything," Aunt Flo said disgustedly.

"I don't agree," Grace said. "I feel she tries to be very honest. Most of us prefer to see things as they should be rather than as they really are. We rationalize and accept rather than question. Marie's generation is not afraid to question. I say that's good."

"They do seem afraid of soap and

water," Aunt Flo sniffed. "Dirty hippies!"

"Only a few of them wear beards and funny clothes," Grace said, "and I can't picture Marie going around with flowers in her hair."

"I can picture her in some dreadful basement with a lot of awful people," the old woman said fretfully. "I can't sleep at night worrying that she might be murdered."

Grace was alarmed. "Don't say anything like that to Dad," she warned.

Aunt Flo at once looked so guilty that she was sure she must have already done so. The old woman drew herself up in a regal fashion. "I think you can depend on me to behave sensibly. I'm not a child, you know."

"Of course not," Grace said, "but Dad does worry a lot. A great deal of the time he keeps it to himself. He did have that mild heart attack three years ago and I don't think any extra annoyance is good for him."

"Adam is my brother," the old woman said. "I think more of him than I do of myself."

"I know that."

"And you two motherless girls have been my equal concern," Aunt Flo went on in a familiar vein. Grace had heard something much like it many times before. She knew the old woman meant to be sincere but doubted that she was quite as selfless as she considered herself.

Grace murmured, "You have always been dear to us."

"I'll never rest until you are both safely married with homes of your own," she continued. "Then I'll feel my work is done."

"But you've never married, Aunt Flo," Grace pointed out with a small smile. "and I'd say you have been very happy."

The old woman looked mildly surprised. "My case is quite different," she said. "Had the young man I was engaged to not died suddenly, I would have married." Grace knew this story as well. But she'd noticed that Aunt Flo had never been anxious to fill in any details of the romance. And no one else seemed to be able to supply any facts.

Grace looked at her wristwatch. "It's getting late," she said. "I must go. I have an appointment."

Aunt Flo's thin lips compressed in a straight line of disapproval. Then she said, "Why are you always in such a rush to get away from me? I do believe you dislike my company."

She shook her head. "You know that's nonsense."

"I'm not so sure," the older woman said, her pale blue eyes regarding Grace with suspicion. "You and Marie take after your mother. She was the same. People and things in Branton were never good enough for her. I wonder she ever stooped to marry a West and come live here."

"Now, you're being unfair," Grace protested. "Mother and Dad were very much in love. I've never known two people who cared for each other as they did. Dad has been only a shadow of himself since her death."

Aunt Flo nodded. "I'm not saying Adam didn't love her. I'm his sister and no one else is closer to him. I know he loved your mother, but I do ask myself if she loved him equally. Her family had lost all its money at the time she married Adam. And I don't think she'd have looked as far as Branton for a husband if she'd had her choice."

Grace stood up. "I really have to go," she said.

Alarm showed in the thin old woman's pale eyes. "I've made you angry," she fretted. "Why do I always have to spoil things!"

"I know you mean well," Grace said with a sigh. "But you just can't get over the fact that Mother stole Dad away from you. You dominated him before that and you'd like to do it again. You're a possessive sister. I suppose chiefly because you're alone."

"That's very hard talk, my dear," the old woman said. "Cruel words for my ears."

"I don't mean them to be," she said, going over and putting a hand on her aunt's shoulder as she touched her lips to her forehead. "I'm only trying to understand you and your motives. I'm sure you didn't hate Mother even if you sometimes sound as if you did."

Aunt Flo showed astonishment. "Hate your mother! I loved her! When she died, I lost my closest friend. Martha was a true lady. And no matter why she married Adam, she made him a good wife. I've always said that!"

Grace smiled at her sadly. "Yes. I believe you always have."

"If you girls only turn out as well," Aunt Flo said, still seated in her chair by the table.

"I'll let you know when Marie gets home," she promised as she turned to leave the veranda.

"Where are you going now in such a hurry?" her aunt wanted to know.

Grace hesitated. It was one of the things she detested about living in a small town. Everyone felt he had a right to share in all you did. Aunt Flo was making her feel like a child and she resented it.

"It's not important," she said.

"Then surely you won't mind telling me," Aunt Flo said stubbornly.

"I'm dropping by Dr. Daniels' place," she said. "We're reading some books together."

"Ray Daniels, indeed!" Aunt Flo exclaimed. "Im sure your father wouldn't approve of that. Ray Daniels has always been a troublemaker! He was so radical in his ideas that the school board retired him as principal of Branton High School two years before his retirement was due!"

"It was because of his health!" Grace protested. "His arthritis is very bad now. He wouldn't be able to get to the school in really bad winter weather."

"I know the polite excuses they made," Aunt Flo said. "But I was a member of the board who acted on his case, so I think I'm familiar with the facts. He was not wanted."

"Then I say the board was short-sighted," Grace said. "I'd call Dr. Daniels an inspired teacher. If he'd chosen to practice his profession anywhere else but in his home town, he'd be revered today."

Aunt Flo nodded. "I know what he's like. Ray Daniels always had a tongue and a way that would charm the dead along with the living. But he's never been able to forget he's not from one of the old families in Branton. He hates us all. In the days before the Second World War

I'm certain he was a Communist."

"A lot of people turned to communism then who wouldn't have anything to do with it now," Grace said. "There seemed no other hope at the time."

"No West turned Communist," Aunt Flo said with obvious pride. "Nor any of Dick Browning's family either. None of the good families in the town thought that way."

"Of course not," Grace said bitterly. "The hard times didn't touch you."

"Does your father know you're visiting Ray Daniels?"

"Yes." Grace didn't mention it, but the revelation of her visits had produced much the same irate response from her father.

"Well, I'm certain he can't be happy about it."

"He feels I'm old enough to make my own decisions," she said.

"Go on reading with that man and you'll wind up as radical-minded as he is," her aunt warned. "Now that he's no longer able to pollute the minds of our high school youngsters, he's reaching out for easy marks such as you."

"I enjoy the time I spend with him," she said defiantly.

Aunt Flo looked especially bleak. "Well, don't say I didn't warn you. Give my love to your father."

"I will. Goodbye, Aunt Flo." It had been another of many disquieting visits with the old woman.

Dr. Ray Daniels lived in a small cedar-shingled cottage on the outskirts of Branton. It was set back from the main highway and had a view of neither the river nor the ocean. But the grounds had been neatly landscaped, and in the rear of the house there was a pleasant little garden sheltered by a tall basketweave wooden fence. It was in the garden that the ailing veteran educator spent every warm afternoon.

He was seated in a weathered chair of wicker and he offered her a smile of greeting without rising as she joined him. "I'm glad you were able to come."

"I meant to get here sooner."

"No hurry," he assured her with a wave of a hand enlarged and twisted by the arthritis that had made him a near-invalid. He had been a big man in his day, but now his bony frame was emaciated. A thatch of unruly white hair topped his kindly lined face, and the eyes behind his heavy rimless glasses were warm and friendly.

"I had lunch with my Aunt Flo," she said. "I'm sure you know her."

"Miss Florence West," the old man said in his harsh voice. "Indeed I do. A lady of very decided opinions."

"Branton opinions," Grace said with disgust. "I think she and my father are two of the most parochial people I know."

The old man's eyes twinkled. "It's true they do measure most things by the town's standards. But then it has done very well by them. So perhaps it's right they should give it loyalty."

"I call it stupidity," she said with bitterness. "Father is really a fine person, and Aunt Flo isn't really bad. But their viewpoints make them narrow and mean."

"I'm not the best one to comment on that," he warned her. "I've always been regarded as a danger to the town's stability."

She gave him a direct look. "Were you really retired from the high school because of your convictions?"

He chuckled. "Well, let's say my ideas put the School Board in a generous frame of mind. I only wonder they took so many years to get around to it."

"So it is true," she fumed. "I almost doubted it."

"I've never been resentful," Dr. Daniels told her. "I was old and tired. Time they put me on the shelf."

She smiled. "You're a long way from that. There's just one thing that puzzles me. Why did you ever remain here? You could have gone anywhere."

The old man hesitated and then gave her an amused glance. "It's a long story. I'll tell you about it one day. Just now we have our book to consider."

They had been reading the plays of Shakespeare. And now they had come to *Twelfth Night*. Dr. Daniels read aloud. When he came to what he considered an especially good line, he would pause and repeat it for her.

"This one," he said, and read, "Foolery, sir, does walk about the orb like the sun;

34

it shines everywhere."

"Indeed it does," Grace agreed with laughter.

"So many of our sayings come from Shakespeare," Grace said. "I didn't realize it until we began reading these plays."

"We lean heavily upon the Bard of Avon," the old scholar said.

They read on and then discussed the play some more. By that time it was nearly five and time for Grace to leave. She stood up and studied the old man with anxious eyes.

"Is there anything I can do before I go?" she asked.

"Not a thing," he assured her as he put the closed copy of the play aside. "In a minute I'll get up and go inside. Because I'm a bachelor of long standing, one of my pet joys is the preparation of my own meals. I fancy myself as a cook. You must join me at dinner one day."

"Only if you'll allow me to help get it ready."

He raised one of the pathetically twisted hands. "Not a chance," he told her. "I'm not a complete invalid yet. I value my independence."

"Thank you," she said. "I'll come back Tuesday."

"Fine," the old teacher said. "If it rains, we can work inside. Though I do prefer it out here when the weather is good."

"So do I," she said. And she bade him a quick goodbye and started on her way. She knew he didn't like to have her stand there and watch his struggles to get to his feet. She had endured it once, and the sight of him battling to rise with the aid of his two canes had made her want to cry.

Now she drove away from Branton again to her own home which was located on the ocean about three miles outside the city. It was a huge red brick building which her grandfather had built to replace the first wooden mansion. It was reputed to be much uglier than the original building in appearance, but her grandfather had considered it a good deal safer. The grounds surrounding it were ample with a number of wooden outbuildings. They kept a small staff of servants to operate the house and care for the land. The house staff was headed by a veteran Swedish couple, Mr. Paul Olsen and his wife Hilda.

When Grace reached the house, Hilda Olsen met her at the front door. She was a big, bony woman with a friendly smile. "Your father was asking for you, Miss Grace," she said. "He's gone out to the garden for a stroll before dinner."

"I'll find him," Grace said.

She discovered him standing by a tall elm tree to the right of the house. He was busily engaged in staring up at one of its branches. As she came up to him, he glanced at her. "See that," he said. "We've got a large dead branch that ought to be removed."

"I noticed it only the other day," she said. "This tree always seemed so healthy."

"We'll have the tree surgeon give an opinion on it," Adam West said. He was wearing a gray business suit that set off his distinguished figure. Now he placed an arm around Grace and kissed her. "Did you see your Aunt Flo?"

"Yes," she said, as they strolled toward

the rose bushes that lined this section of the gravel path. "I had lunch with her."

Her father's serious face showed a flicker of amusement as he glanced at her. "You don't sound too enthusiastic about it."

She made a face. "You know how difficult Aunt Flo can be when she likes."

"We should be considerate to those older than ourselves," he reminded her. "And Florence is my older sister."

"I was nice to her," Grace explained hastily. "But I was glad to have an excuse to get away."

"Did she mention Marie?"

"You know she never misses doing that."

"What did she say?"

"That she worries about Marie," Grace said carefully. "And she wanted to know the exact hour and minute when she'd be back. Of course I couldn't tell her. So at once she began accusing me of not liking her."

Adam West chuckled. "She was always touchy on that score."

"It was pretty ridiculous," Grace said.

And she stopped. "There is something I should tell you about Marie."

"Oh?" Her father's patrician features took on a worried frown. He let his arm drop from around her and stood facing her. "What is it?"

"I think I should tell you because Aunt Flo almost pried it out of me this afternoon," she explained. "And I wouldn't want her to find out first."

"Go on, please," her father said with a brisk irritation.

"It's Marie," she said awkwardly. "She's coming home because she's planning to be married."

"To be married!" Her father echoed the words in surprise. "This is all something new, isn't it?"

"Not really," she said. "Marie's mentioned it in several of her letters. But it was only in the last one she was really definite."

"I see," Adam West said with a deep sigh. "I suppose it's that fellow she's been seeing so much of. That Michael Blair!"

"It is Michael," she admitted. "I hope you're not too upset."

"I'm not pleased," he said. "I wish Marie had come to her senses. I thought she might be over this madness when she wrote she was coming home. Of course, I had no idea this was behind it."

"He's coming down with her."

"She's bringing him to Branton?"

"Yes."

"She might have spared us that." Adam West spoke in a bitter tone.

"He may not be so bad. He's college educated with a degree of some kind."

"He hasn't been putting it to much use then," Adam West said angrily. "Holing up in some filthy tenement basement. What kind of a man can he be?"

"You've picked a lot of those ideas up from Aunt Flo," she said. "You know how she dotes on the worst of the tabloids. I'm positive the truth about Marie and this Mike is not really so shocking as you imagine."

Her father stared at her for a moment of silent amazement. "You sound very sure of that. Has she told you anything to indicate they're living on a better scale than the rest of the East Village flower people?"

"Not really," she admitted.

"Then don't take too rose-colored a view of the situation," he warned. "My worry is that he and Marie are both taking some kind of drug. I can't think why she'd put up with that wretchedness there otherwise."

"She might if she had a very strong desire to be free," Grace said.

Adam West looked startled. "Free of what?"

"Of you and me. The house and the town for that matter," Grace explained. "She isn't nearly as patient and yielding as I am. Yet I think I can understand and sympathize with her."

Her father frowned. "I hardly expected to hear you take sides against me in this."

"I think you should know how I feel," she said.

"Are you telling me you aren't satisfied with your life here either? That you regret your engagement to Dick Browning?"

"I'd rather not discuss that side of it," she told him. "Just let's say you haven't allowed either Marie or me very much freedom."

41

"I see," he said in a dry tone. He stared at her a moment. "I'm afraid you've picked a bad time to bring this up."

She looked up at his weary face. So there had been something else bothering him. She said, "Why do you say that?"

"Because it's true. Dick is joining us here for dinner. We're facing some trouble at the plant and I want to talk things over after our meal. He should be here by now."

" What's wrong at the plant?" she asked.

"We could be facing a walkout," Adam West said.

"A walkout?" she was surprised.

"That's right. For sometime there has been agitation for a union. I've managed to settle it each time it came up. But some of the key men have gone on organizing and contacting a national group."

"But I don't understand," she said. "Hasn't the plant had a union right along?"

"We've had our own organization," her father said carefully. "It's a purely local affair. More a group to protect the men's

42

rights than a strict union. But it has cost them nothing in dues, and I've accepted it as a proper bargaining agency. Now they want to strike out against me."

"In other words, they want to form a regular union branch with national affiliations."

"That's about it," her father said. "Another sign of the times. They'll gain nothing and pay dearly for the privilege."

"Won't they be stronger as a bargaining group if they're part of a national union?" she asked.

"They think so. It's an illusion," her father said harshly. "Any extra money they get from me will go to the union in dues. I'm going to fight it."

She was saved from making a reply by the appearance of Dick Browning. Her husband-to-be came toward them with a vigorous step. He was wearing a dark suit with a pin stripe that enhanced his youthful, crew-cut good looks. He was light complected with deep-set blue eyes and a broad, determined face.

"Just got away," he told her father as he joined them. He smiled at her and kissed her lightly on the lips. "At least some good comes out of this headache. We have dinner together," he said. And then he handed a newspaper to her father. "There's a photo of the union man. I got this paper from one of the boys."

Her father studied the photo in the opened paper. "A stranger to me," he said.

Grace glanced at the photo and at once felt stunned. For the man shown there was no stranger to her. He was Mabel's cousin whom she'd met only that morning — Geoff Bailey!

3

ADAM WEST scowled at the photo. "So this fellow is a nephew of Fred Bailey's," he observed.

"That's right," Dick Browning said. "I understand he arrived in Branton last night. He talked at the hotel with some of the union agitators from the plant when he first got here. But he doesn't seem to be in a hurry to come and see us."

Grace's father handed the newspaper back to Dick. "I'm not surprised," he said in his dry fashion. "I gave him to understand we weren't interested in any dealings with him. I made it clear in my last letter."

Dick looked somewhat startled. "I didn't know you'd engaged in any personal correspondence with him, sir."

"He wrote me directly after receiving your official reply," Adam West said blandly. "I let him know that our true position was even stronger than the one you'd expressed on behalf of the board."

Dick nodded. "I see," he said quietly. "Then he's probably decided there isn't any use wasting time with management in this problem."

"I hope he has," Adam West said with something like a sneer showing on his patrician face. "I have no time for people of his ilk."

"The only adverse result of that, sir," the crew-cut Dick said seriously, "is that it may goad our people to more extremes. They'll be apt to feel frustrated from the start if there seems no opportunity of a hearing."

"Better they know the truth from the first," said Adam West harshly. "We have done well by the workers in our plant."

Grace was so caught up in the conversation and troubled by its course that she couldn't resist bursting out with, "I've met Geoff Bailey and I don't think you should underestimate him. He seems a person of tremendous power."

"Well," her father said at last, his cold gray eyes fixed on her. "I must say this is interesting. Where did you meet Bailey?"

"At the Country Club this morning," she said.

Her father's eyebrows lifted. "He must indeed be a hardworking union leader," he said, "spending his mornings at the Country Club. I doubt if he'll do much on this mission if he keeps to that schedule."

Dick gave a curt laugh. "It does sound promising," he agreed. "Better for him to be there than down at the plant."

"I still say you shouldn't sell him short," Grace advised the two men. "He's no ordinary type."

"Of course not," her father said with one of his bleak, stubborn expressions on his aristocratic face. Then he turned to Dick and in a brisk manner said, "Time to go in and enjoy a martini before dinner."

Grace followed the two men inside and left them in the big living room while she went on upstairs to freshen up and change for the evening meal. Before-dinner martinis had long been a tradition with her father, and he wasn't one to depart from tradition even on an evening like this when trouble was in the air.

Dick's general behavior in the garden

had left Grace with a sense of uneasiness. For one thing, he seemed much too ready to bow to her father. She was glad that he got on well with her dad but she would have liked to have had him express more opinions of his own. She was sure Dick had a good mind and was capable of putting on a better show. It would be tragic if he had become content to be a yes-man for her father.

Tragic not only for Dick but for her father and the business as well. No matter what her father might think, Grace had no illusions that Geoff Bailey would make an easy adversary. And it was sheer nonsense for Dick and her dad to think the paternalistic local organization would satisfy the plant workers indefinitely. They were bound to want affiliation with a national group and the security it would bring them in bargaining.

Dick came to her with a glass of sherry when she joined the two by the massive sideboard that had been a family treasure for generations. The first affluent West had purchased it on a visit to London and brought it back. It had been a conversation piece ever since.

Grace took a sip of the bittersweet sherry. "I was listening to you two from the hallway," she said. "You sounded very pleased with yourselves."

Her father's cool glance appraised her. "Do I detect a note of criticism in that remark?"

She smiled over the sherry glass. "Not really. Though I do worry whenever you sound smug."

Dick looked amused. "And you thought we sounded smug now?"

She nodded. "Very much the Establishment boys."

"Now you're talking like Marie," Adam West said sharply. "If I have to be grouped like some sort of animal, I'd much prefer to be classified as one of the Establishment."

"You have a point there, sir," Dick said with his usual deference. "Why must everyone be tagged these days? It leaves no room for individualists."

Grace gave her fiance a knowing glance. "But then there are so very few individualists left!"

Dick's broad face took on a faint

crimson shade. "I hadn't noticed," he said in a tone less sure.

"I wouldn't expect you to," she said by way of reproval and dismissal. Then she turned to her father and added, "I think Marie's quarrel with the Establishment is that they've held the lead so long they've gone stale. They're no longer fitted to show the way because they simply don't want to go anywhere."

Adam West's grimly distinguished features showed nothing but scorn for her words. "Often it's better to preserve order and dignity than submit to so-called progress."

"Agreed," she said. "But when all action is frozen, there has to be a change."

Her father gave her a bleak smile. "So you'd have me grow a beard and wear flowers in my hair and write long poems of love about my fellow man."

"You're deliberately caricaturing all that I'm trying to defend," she said. "If the hippies are being too exuberant, so are you. Both sides are using the excesses of the other to prove their point."

"You play such an excellent game of

golf and look so lovely, I wonder why you try to settle the world's problems," her father said with familiar irony. "I suggest we go in to dinner."

Hilda Olsen served an excellent dinner as usual. Grace found herself left out of much of the conversation between Dick and her father. She deliberately said little since she felt her parent had rebuked her for expressing her opinions earlier. She had no wish to upset him at a time when he was having extra problems at the plant. And also Marie could arrive any day with the young man she proposed to marry. This news had not gone too well with her father, and Grace was sure there would be a scene when Marie showed up with Mike.

They returned to the living room after dinner where the business talk between Dick and her father continued over brandy and cigars. It was after nine, and dusk was setting in before Adam West excused himself, saying that he was going up to his room to do some postponed reading, and finally left the two young people alone.

Dick still hadn't shed his awkwardness

even though her father had gone upstairs. Coming over to stand before the divan on which she had seated herself, he said, "How about a stroll in the garden?"

"If you'd like it," she said, rising.

"It is a warm evening," Dick said, and with an appreciative smile he added, "Have I told you how wonderful you look?"

"Not until now," she said with an arch glance. "You were too busy paying attention to Dad."

"Take it easy, Grace," he begged. "You've been sniping at me all evening!"

"Have I?" she inquired too innocently.

"You know it!" he said, taking her by the arm. "Let's go outside where I can cool off."

The garden was pleasant in the coolness of the dusk. The air was filled with a mixed perfume of the many flowers, the pungent odor of evergreens, and a tang of the nearby ocean to give it all a special zest. They strolled hand in hand.

"Why were you so vindictive toward me tonight?" Dick asked.

"Don't worry about it," she said. "I'm a girl of moods."

"There was more to it than that," he insisted.

She glanced at him, unable to see his expression clearly in the fading light. "You did bob and scrape like a personable little puppet every time Dad pulled the string."

He halted and, facing her, said with some exasperation. "Look here! Your father is my superior in the firm and a good deal older than I am. I owe him some respect."

"But not your self-respect," she protested. "There must be some happy place to draw the line."

"I think I know it."

"I saw no evidence of it tonight," she argued. "I think he's all wrong about this union business. And you must if you have any sense at all. Yet you agreed with him!"

Dick faced her in the shadows. "I don't suppose a good-looking man named Geoff Bailey has anything to do with your sudden interest in unions," he snapped. "You seemed pretty excited about being introduced to him!"

"Why do you say that?"

"You said he was impressive and suggested power. It added up to the fact you admired him," Dick accused her.

"You make that sound like some sort of crime!" she exclaimed.

"I don't think it's right for you to take sides against your father and me!"

"I have a right to my opinions," she said.

"And I don't like being measured up against a stranger," Dick told her angrily. "You did nothing but sulk all evening."

With a deep sigh she said, "Let's not argue any more, darling!"

Dick hesitated. "Sorry," he said. "I didn't mean to start anything. But all at once I had to get it off my chest."

She touched his arm. "I suppose I did behave badly. But only because I'm worried. Worried about Dad, what's liable to happen at the plant, and most of all about you."

"About me?" he sounded mildly incredulous. "What is there to bother you about me?"

"I'm afraid of you losing yourself," she said. "Before you became manager, and before we were engaged, you seemed such a different person. So much more self-reliant. So ready to express your own opinions and not echo Father's! Has working for Dad done this to you? Being engaged to me made this change? If so, it's wrong!"

"I'm not aware that I have changed," he protested.

"You have," she assured him. "You've become a very careful young man. And I don't like you in the role."

He spread his hands. "Suppose I have tried to be agreeable to your dad? What's wrong with wanting to please him? He's done a lot for me, and I'm going to be his son-in-law."

"You're going to be my husband," she corrected him. "And the only way you can hope to hold my respect and Father's is to stand by your own opinions. Go back to being what you were when we first met."

He studied her in silence before he said, "You're harping a lot on respect. Doesn't love enter into our relationship?"

"Of course."

"It doesn't seem to count much with you, right now," he said with meaning.

"Aren't you in love with me anymore, Grace?"

"I think so."

"What kind of an answer is that?" he demanded, reaching out and taking her by the arms.

She looked up into the strong face blurred by darkness. "Sometimes I wonder if I know what love really is," she faltered. "If there is enough between us to justify a marriage."

"I can only speak for myself," he told her quietly as he drew her toward him. "I love you, Grace. I love you more than anything else." And he gave her no opportunity to reply since he pressed his lips against hers for a lasting kiss.

She enjoyed the solace of his embrace. And she had no doubts that his love for her was real enough. At least it seemed real to him. Yet it would be impossible for her to make him realize what she was worrying about or to see himself as she saw him. She could only hope that she was being unfair to him and would gradually come to know this. That she would be able to settle for what they had of romance and not strive for an impossible ideal. Life, she had learned, was almost entirely a bitter compromise.

When Dick finally released her, he said, "I'll have to leave soon. We'll be operating on borrowed time from now on. The staff may decide to walk off any day."

"Can't you reason with Dad?" she asked him. "He might listen to you. I think you should try to get him to at least consider the proposals for a new union."

"He doesn't like me to cross him in these things."

"He has made you manager."

"Under his direction."

"But you do have a lot of authority," she said. "More than anyone else. I believe he'd listen to you."

"It wouldn't do any good," Dick complained. "He'd hear me out and then do exactly as he liked."

"For me," Grace begged. "Try this for me. I only want you to place all the facts fairly before him. You owe it to yourself to do that."

"All right," he said evasively. "I'll try."

"Promise me you will."

"I promise," he said wearily. "Why make so much of it?"

"Because it means a great deal to me. And I think it will to you in due time."

He took her in his arms again. "If I'm weak sometimes," he said, "it's only because I'm afraid of losing you."

"Being weak could be the surest way to do it," she warned him.

"I'll remember that," he promised as he kissed her again.

Grace awoke the following morning in a much better mood. She had an early breakfast and went straight to the Country Club. Jamie was waiting for her and she and the dour little pro played a sharp eighteen holes leaving her the winner by an ample number of points.

"You're a bonnie lassie," Jamie chuckled as he escorted her to her car. "You'll be doing me credit in the July tournament."

She gave him a rueful smile as she swung in behind the wheel of the white convertible. "I'm beginning to wonder if being a tournament winner is all that important."

The little Scotsman looked shocked. "That's sacrilegious!" he announced solemnly.

"Winning silver trophies for the club is hardly a life goal," she told him.

"Maybe not in your opinion," Jamie said stoutly, "but it is in mine. You're the pride of the entire club, and they'll no take it well if ye let us down."

She smiled. "I'll try not to forget that," she said as she switched on the engine. "I'll see you tomorrow morning."

She went straight back home and was surprised to see her father had not left for the plant. Instead he was standing talking to the gardener when she drove up. He waved to her and then went on with his earnest conversation.

Grace got out of the convertible and strolled across the lawn to join him. He was wearing dark slacks and a fawn pullover sweater over a white shirt open at the neck and looked very handsome and almost youthful in spite of his graying hair. He said, "I'm waiting for the tree surgeon. He promised me he'd come out this morning, and I want to be here when he arrives."

She glanced over at the tree with the dead area. "But he'll do just as well whether you're here or not," she said.

"I prefer to be here," he said coldly.

Grace took the hint. It meant there was to be no reasoning with him. He intended to do as he pleased. So often that was his attitude. She thought it dated back to the death of her mother and the heartbreak he'd experienced then. It had turned him into a cold, bitter man. Knowing this, she was moved to sympathy rather than anger.

She said, "It's such a lovely morning and you're so seldom here I thought we might take the boat out." Her father had a new thirty-foot cabin cruiser which they used very little.

He shook his head. "Some other day."

"You always say that," she told him. "But we never do seem to get any good out of the new boat. Why?"

"I think it's perfectly obvious. I told you I plan to be here when the tree surgeon arrives."

"I can't imagine why you spent all that money on the boat!" she exclaimed.

"We have it to use when we wish," he

said in his calm, overbearing way.

The unreasonableness of his stand began to anger her. With a toss of her head she told him, "All right. I'll go out on the water myself. I'll take Paul's boat." Paul was the Swedish handyman, and his boat was an antiquated wooden motor launch. He had given her permission to use it any time she liked.

As she started away, her father called after her. "Grace, I wish you wouldn't!"

She halted to turn on him coldly. "Why not?"

"It's not safe for you to be out alone in that old boat."

"You won't take me in the new one," she said. "At least let me have a little enjoyment on my own."

"Maybe we can go out this afternoon if Marie doesn't show up or there's no trouble at the plant," her father suggested.

"Sorry. I don't care to wait," she said with a cutting sarcasm in her tone. And she wheeled around and hurried away in the direction of their private dock.

Within a few minutes she had cast off from the wharf, and the old boat was heading gamely away from shore. Grace quickly forgot her annoyance in the pleasure of the sparkling silver waves, the breeze streaking through her auburn hair and the general feeling of freedom which standing at the controls of the ancient craft gave her.

There were several other boats in her general area, and as the old motor roared out and she passed them, she offered them a friendly wave. It was the odd sound of the motor that attracted her attention a few minutes later. An erratic sound she'd never heard before. She glanced down at the engine and, to her horror, saw the spurt of flame from it. A flame that was extending all along the path of the narrow gas line.

Her pretty face contorted with fear as she recognized the boat was on fire. A fire that had gained enough headway to place her in deadly danger. Even now it was racing to the gas tank. She screamed and edged way, allowing the controls to go free so that the craft veered madly. Smoke rose high now along with the flames, and as she prepared to leap over the side, the explosion came!

4

A ROUGH, male voice said, "That's Adam West's girl you fished out of the ocean!"

Another male voice with a more familiar ring said quietly, "Yes, I know."

They came through to Grace in a blurred kind of way. She stirred and opened her eyes and found herself staring up into the concerned face of Geoff Bailey. He was dressed in rough clothes, his shirt open at the neck, and he looked more manly and handsome than ever.

"You!" she said.

He nodded with a faint smile. "That's right. We keep meeting. I was afraid you'd suffered some kind of concussion."

She frowned. And then remembrance came rushing back and she raised herself excitedly on an elbow. "The boat!"

"You needn't worry," he said, placing a restraining hand on her arm.

She glanced into his handsome, bronzed

63

face and then out at the water. "What happened?"

"The boat blew up. Luckily we were close enough to pick you up."

Grace looked at him again and shivered. For the first time she realized she was drenched and miserably cold. "What about the boat?"

He raised his eyebrows. "An oil slick on the waves and some bits of debris. I guess you have a claim on your insurance company."

"It wasn't my boat," she said, clasping her elbows now that complete nervous reaction had set in and she was trembling and her teeth chattering. She gave more attention to him. "You're all wet, too!" she commented.

"I had to go in for you," he said with proper modesty. "I couldn't reach you from the deck of this fishing boat."

Now she took in more of her surroundings and the several hardy-looking young men standing in the background. She told him, "This is one of the boats that supplies Dad's plant."

Geoff smiled at her good-naturedly.

"You come up with all the right answers," he said.

"What are you doing on it?"

"I came out to get an idea of the operation," he said. "I take an interest in these things."

She eyed him reprovingly. "I know why. I've heard all about you and why you came to Branton."

He didn't seem abashed by her news. "Good," he said. "Saves a lot of involved explanations."

"My dad!" she gasped. "He was watching me from the shore. I wonder if he saw what happened."

Geoff nodded toward the wharf. "Looks a lot like it," he said.

She followed his glance and saw that her dad was standing out at the very edge of the wharf along with two or three others. She was reasonably certain one of them was the gardener and guessed the stour figure belonged to Paul Olsen.

"Poor Paul!" she mourned. "How will I ever explain about his boat."

"He had a fine visual explanation," Geoff Bailey said.

"You make it sound a joke!" she said

with a hint of anger.

He shook his head. "Sorry, I didn't mean to. I have a habit of taking things lightly even when I'm upset."

They were nearing the wharf now, and she could see that her father was badly shaken. As the fishing boat grated to a halt against the wharf, Geoff helped her to her feet and then assisted her in getting up the ladder. In a moment she was in her father's arms with Geoff standing by.

"Foolish girl!" Adam West said in an emotion-choked voice as he held her close to him. "I warned you against that boat."

Her face was buried against him. "I'm sorry, Dad."

Her father addressed himself to Geoff Bailey. "It seems I owe you a great debt," he said stiffly. "I saw you go into the water and save Grace."

"There was no danger involved," Geoff said.

"I'd say differently," her father told the young man.

"The main thing was that she jumped out of the boat before the full force of the explosion," Geoff said. "It was her own quick thinking that saved her life."

Grace pulled away from her father and turned to Geoff with a wan smile. "You're being entirely too modest," she said, and held out her hand. "I'm very grateful."

He took her hand and held it for a long moment as their eyes met. "I'm glad I was there," he said simply.

Grace turned to her father. "I don't believe you two know each other."

But Adam West was not in a friendly humor. "I know Mr. Bailey by reputation," he said. "And we've corresponded."

"So we have!" Geoff said genially enough. "I'm glad we've finally met, Mr. West."

"That was almost inevitable now that you've come to Branton," Adam West said in his cold way.

"I hope we'll have more meetings," Geoff went on.

"I very much doubt that," her father said grimly.

Geoff didn't seem put out at all. He turned to her. "Better take a warm shower as soon as you can," he suggested. "I

67

wouldn't want you to catch a cold and have to miss the Country Club dance." He didn't wait for an answer but left with a nod and a smile.

Grace turned to her father. "You weren't particularly friendly to him. He saved my life."

"Don't remind me. I deeply resent being in his debt."

"Must you be so hateful. It's only a business difference between you," she said. "I think you're taking this much too seriously."

"We can discuss this in privacy later."

Turning to the stout, bald Paul Olsen, she said, "I'm so sorry, Mr. Olsen. I'll pay you for your boat."

The old servant's fat face showed a grin. "No harm done as long as you're safe, Miss Grace."

"I will get you a new boat," she promised.

"She was insured," Paul Olsen told her. "Don't you worry yourself about her."

Her father put an arm around her and insisted she return to the house at once. Hilda Olsen was waiting for her and bustled about helping her undress and insisted she take a warm bath rather than a shower.

The old woman stood grimly by. "You came near your death, Miss Grace."

"It's the cold water I minded most," she said with a smile from the bathtub.

Grace felt better after her bath. Her spirits and nerves were returning to normal. Wearing a dressing gown over her pajamas she went down to the living room for a while. It was there she was joined by her father.

Adam West eyed her. "Are you certain I shouldn't call a doctor?"

"No need to do that," she said. "I'm fine."

He sighed. "Can you imagine how I felt as I watched your accident from the shore?"

"I know. I'm sorry."

"You realize I would have blamed myself if you'd been killed. I would have felt it could have been avoided if I'd taken you out in the other boat as you asked."

"It doesn't matter now," she told him.

"I think it does," he said. "I warned you Paul's boat wasn't safe."

"I'd used it so often before."

"But always at a risk," he said. "I hope it will teach you not to disobey me. When I tell you something, it is usually for your own good."

"But you persist in treating me like a child," she protested. "And you did the same thing with Marie. You're so unbending, you drive us from you."

"I have to do double parent duty for you girls," he reminded her. "I don't want to be accused of neglecting you."

"If you would just let us learn by our own mistakes," Grace said. "I know we'd be a lot happier."

He stared at her for another moment of silence. "You're feeling so much better I suppose you'll be going to the club for the dance tonight?"

"Yes," she said. "Dick is calling for me."

"See that you stay with Dick," her father said sternly.

"What do you mean by that?"

"We both heard what Geoff Bailey said on the wharf," her father reminded her.

"And we both know he's planning to see you at the dance."

"Of course."

"Stay away from him."

"I'll have to be friendly," she protested. "He did save my life. And anyway, I like him."

"Bailey would have rescued anyone who was in the water. So don't take it so personally."

"I still don't know why you hate him so," she told him.

"Why do you think he was on that fishing boat?" Adam West demanded.

Grace shrugged. "He said he was studying its operation."

"Of course he was," Adam West snapped. "He was out there collecting data to use against me and the firm."

"It is his job," she said firmly. "Why regard him as a criminal for trying to do it?"

"You don't know much about unions and their links with the Mafia and other gangster elements," her father argued. "I don't want that kind of affiliation for my employees."

"You're telling only one side of the

story," Grace argued. "There are plenty of honest unions. In fact the majority of them are. So why try to keep your people from the benefits they offer?"

"I don't consider you qualified to argue about unions with me," her father said. "And I repeat. Stay away from Geoff Bailey at the dance."

"I'm sorry. I won't promise that, Dad."

"You'd prefer to humiliate me?"

"I think I can promise not to do that."

"If you fraternize with Bailey, you'll be hurting me and our cause."

"Is that all, Dad?" she asked.

"That's all," he said.

She left him and went on up to her own room. Because Grace had a deep love for her father and knew all his other wonderful qualities, she felt his present mood was especially tragic. His embittered attitude had begun with her mother's death, and now he seemed to be yearly getting more conservative and set in his ways.

The balance of the day passed without event. Her father had little to say at dinner. Afterward she went into the living room to play the stereo while he made a visit to the grounds to inspect the elm on which the tree surgeon had worked that afternoon. She selected a popular dance record, and it had just begun to play when the stereo went dead. After fiddling with the various controls for several minutes, she gave it up as a bad job. Picking up a magazine from several set out on a table, she sat down in a wing-back chair and began to read.

She was still reading when Dick Browning came into the room. He looked very handsome in dark trousers and silk sports jacket and a crimson shade along with a black bow tie. He advanced towards Grace with an expression of concern on his broad young face

"What's this I hear about you nearly being drowned?" he asked.

She smiled and put the magazine aside. "It's greatly exaggerated," she said, rising.

"Not the way I heard it. The boat was wrecked."

"I'm fine as you can see," she said lightly.

"You should have listened to your father," he worried. "You're too ready to take chances."

"You needn't repeat the lecture," she told him. "I had it first hand from Dad."

"Awkward that Geoff Bailey had to show up at that exact time," Dick said, his face shadowed.

She raised her eyebrows. "I'd say it was lucky that he did."

"Sure! But I wish it had been anyone else besides him!"

"I don't think it's important enough to worry about," she said. And wanting to change the subject, she told him about the stereo. She went over to it and showed him what had happened. "It seemed to burn out," she explained.

Dick gave his attention to the silence machine for a few minutes, probing into its walnut elegance. "It needs a professional's attention. I have a man at the plant who's a whizz at this stuff. He does all kinds of repairs for us."

"You mean that Joe Spear?" she asked.

Dick looked amazed. "That's the fellow," he said. "Do you know him?"

She nodded. "Yes. You sent him here before to install the color television and the special antenna. I met him then."

"I guess I did have him do that," Dick recalled. "I'd forgotten. Then you know he's an expert on electronics."

"He seemed very clever," Grace agreed. "But I don't like to bother you with this. It doesn't seem fair to rob the plant of a man. I can hire a regular repair man from the village." The truth was she'd resented Joe Spear's overbearing manner when he'd been at the house before. He'd shown a certain aggressiveness she hadn't liked. And she'd received the impression that along with his genius for electronics he had inherited an erratic streak. She felt having him in the house had been a mistake.

"It's no trouble," Dick assured her. "Just leave it to me. I'll have Joe come here first thing on Monday."

She knew there was no use arguing with him or trying to explain her feelings about the brash Joe Spear. So she made a mental note to be out of the house when the young man came to make the repairs on the stereo. And if he did catch her in by accident, she would remain upstairs and away from the possibility of another embarrassing conversation with him.

Dick glanced at his wristwatch, "I guess it's time to leave."

The Country Club was located on the ocean. It was a ten-minute drive from Grace's home and on the outskirts of Branton. It was the only club in the small city and served both the residents and the large influx of summer people whose homes dotted the shore. Many of the summer visitors had already arrived, and so when she and Dick entered the main lounge, it was well filled. Almost automatically she glanced around for a sign of Geoff Bailey but didn't see him.

When they went into the other room with its ring of table and center dance floor, it was apparent that the majority of the tables had been taken. Then from a table on the ocean side of the room a youngish man with horn-rimmed glasses and receding black hair stood and waved to them. She recognized him as Barney Wells, office manager of her father's plant. Gail Wells, his plump blonde wife, was with him, and she was smiling for them to come over.

"Barney wants us to join him and Gail," Dick said. "Okay?"

"I suppose so," she said with a sigh. "There aren't many tables." She wasn't enthusiastic since she knew it would mean listening to an endless tirade from Gail about the woes of caring for her four small children. And since Barney Wells was noted for fawning on his superiors, she would also have to endure his catering to Dick to the point of satire.

"Barney and Gail are swell people," he said defensively.

"I agree," she said in complete surrender as she allowed him to lead her to the table.

It turned out almost exactly as she'd predicted. The four of them sat through most of the music, missing the fun of the other dancing couples. Dick gave her a brief opening dance, and then Barney had made a great show of squiring her out for a short turn around the floor. But the music had changed to a South American beat and he'd begged out, too eager to get back to the table and pour exaggerated praise into Dick's ear. The little man with the horn-rimmed glasses was determined to be in the same camp with her father and Dick.

"We've got to stand pat and show this Bailey he can't break the local organization," Barney said very seriously.

"That is Mr. West's idea," Dick agreed. "But Bailey has gotten to the men, and we'll have to be prepared for some trouble. A strike is almost a certainty."

"I'm betting on you and Mr. West," Barney said with overdone sincerity.

The pleasure of the music was being drowned out by the mundane talk and Grace was wondering why they came to the Country Club at all. These familiar topics could just as well have been gone over at home. Then someone passed by her chair and a familiar voice said. "As I remember, you promised me a dance."

She looked up and saw that it was Geoff Bailey in white dinner jacket and smiling. She said, "I owe you a dance whether it was promised or not."

But this time Dick had turned with a look of angry surprise. Geoff nodded to him and said, "I know you won't refuse me the pleasure."

Dick's reply was a mumbled something that could have been either agreement or refusal. Grace didn't worry that it was indistinct as she rose, smiling, to join the tall Geoff.

As they moved easily to the good beat of the orchestra, Geoff said, "I've been watching you. You've hardly been on the floor all evening. Don't you like to dance?"

She looked up at him. "I'm very fond of it. But the others don't seem so keen."

"You dance well," he said. "I like the club and the orchestra."

"I'm glad," she said. "Do you plan on being in Branton long?"

"That depends," he said, whirling her around lightly. "I'd say I'll likely be here for another Saturday night or two."

"I see," she said.

"You almost said that with a sigh. Why?"

"I was thinking if you plan to be here that long, it means you're expecting delays in organizing your union."

"Don't you approve of my being here awhile?"

"I'm glad you're here," she said. "But I'm worried at the prospect of a battle between you and my father."

"I wouldn't be," he said easily. "It doesn't have to happen."

"Father is planning for it. And so are his key executives."

"Then let them worry. We'll enjoy the music."

The music changed to a waltz and then a cha-cha. Geoff proved himself adept in both rhythms. She enjoyed being in his arms. And when the orchestra played its chord to announce the end of the dance set, she felt a distinct regret.

"I don't want to go back to Cousin Mabel yet," he confessed. "Can't we both play truant and go out for a stroll on the veranda?"

"She'll wonder what happened to you."

"Mabel always finds someone to gossip with," Geoff said.

Grace thought of Dick and Barney in rapt discussion of plant business and Gail waiting to pounce on her with new data on the care of raising of her progeny. And she realized she'd had more than enough.

She linked her arm in Geoff's. "Some fresh air would probably do us both good," she said.

It was quite cool on the veranda, so it was fairly deserted. There was a moon, but it was almost obscured by clouds. She stood at the railing and stared out over the ocean that looked so calm now.

With a tiny shiver she said, "I might be lost somewhere out there but for you."

"Are you cold?" he asked, placing an arm around her protectively as they stood side by side.

She shook her head and looked up at him. "I'm just beginning to realize what a narrow escape I had."

"It's over," he said. "Enjoy the moment and the evening."

Grace gave him a wondering look. "That's your philosophy, isn't it?"

"Living for the moment? Yes," he agreed. "Don't you approve?"

"I'm not sure," she said. "Aren't you grouping yourself with the hedonists?

Living solely for pleasure."

"That's your Puritan New England blood talking. The Baileys are tainted in the same way. I've had to fight it," he told her with a laugh. "But don't worry. I'm no hedonist. I merely believe in living without needless emphasis on the past or too much worry about the future."

"I'm not sure I understand," she admitted.

"It isn't altogether clear to me," he said cheerfully. "But my credo is to try and select the best portions of life and concentrate on them. Just the same as I would in selecting a fine meal. In that way I hope to build constructively."

"It sounds radical and promising."

"It frees me of always bowing to convention," he told her. "And it helps me in making decisions. For instance, when I met you, I knew you were the kind of girl I could easily fall in love with."

And he caught her completely off guard by taking her in his arms and kissing her. It wasn't an unpleasant moment, and she found herself easily surrendering to him. It was when they parted that she was really shocked. Standing in one of the doorways from the lounge was Dick Browning with a look of anger on his broad face. Without a word the crew-cut young man whose engagement ring she wore turned and went back inside.

5

THERE was a moment of silence. Then Geoff said, "Sorry."

She turned to look up at his handsome face. "I wonder if you really are?"

He met her gaze. "My answer should be honest."

"Yes."

"Probably I hoped something like this would happen," he admitted.

The orchestra began to play again inside. She shook her head at him in mock despair. "You've incorrigible! You don't care whom or what you upset."

"I told you I'd been watching you all evening," he reminded her. "And I wasn't impressed with the way your escort was treating you."

"We know each other so well. We've been engaged almost a year. Dick doesn't have to pay court to me. I mean, every minute of the time, he doesn't. We take each other for granted."

"How unromantic," was Geoff's ironic reply.

She frowned. "Not necessarily." But she knew she was making the effort of a defense because she felt she should. Geoff had hit on a weak point in her relationship with the man she planned to marry. Dick could be dreadfully dull at times as he had been tonight. And he subjected her to other dull people which didn't help.

"If there's so little spark in your romance now, what is it going to be like after you've been married a year or two?" Geoff wanted to know.

It was something she preferred not to think about. She was sure, or at least she had partly convinced herself, that with their own home and family she and Dick would find many more things in common, that their lives would continue to grow and they would have a richness to share. It would be different from the uneasy bond between them now.

She said, "We will make out. Don't try to come here and blast people's lives along with our way of life."

He smiled faintly. "Don't you think

your emotions need some stirring? You're drifting into an unsuitable marriage without trying to help yourself. It's time someone took an interest in you and your future."

"You've just about fixed my future," she told him. "How am I going to explain that kiss to Dick?"

Geoff laughed. "Tell him I'm a cad. That I took advantage of you."

"It's close to the truth!"

"He'll be anxious to believe it," he assured her. "You'll have no problem with him."

She sighed. "I don't know what to think of you."

"Believe that I'm your friend."

"I want to," she said seriously, studying him. "I really do."

He touched her arm. "And I'd like to think I fished you out of the ocean for better fate than that table of four."

She smiled. "I'll have to get back to that table of four. And at once. If they'll have me!"

"They'll have you," he promised. "It was fun. I hope we meet soon again."

"Don't count on it," she told him.

"Dick is the jealous type. If I'm able to square tonight I'll be very careful from now on. Goodbye, Geoff."

"Goodnight," he said, amending her goodbye.

She hurried inside without looking back and went straight to the table where Dick was again seated with Gail and Barney Wells. The plump blonde woman gave her a wise smile.

"So you're back at last! Dick said he couldn't find you."

"We stepped outside for some air," she said seating herself.

Gail Wells winked broadly. "If I could find me a man like that, I'd take a stroll on the veranda with him quick!"

Dick caught this sly comment of his friend's wife and turned to Grace unhappily. "Let's dance. It must be almost the last one," he said.

They went out on the crowded floor and almost the first couple they passed was Geoff and Mabel. Mabel smiled and spoke to them, and Geoff nodded in his quiet fashion.

Dick swiftly turned her away from the other two and they kept on dancing. "He has a nerve," he raged.

"Let's not talk about it now," she begged. "Isn't the music good?"

"You'd think so," the crew-cut young man said sarcastically. "I expect you're in an ecstatic mood!"

"Dick!" she pleaded.

"Bailey or not, he's proven he's not a gentleman," Dick stormed. "Abusing his privilege as a guest of the club."

"You're making a fuss about nothing," she said in his ear.

But he kept on complaining all through the dance until the very end. They said brief goodnights to Barney and Gail and then went out to find Dick's car. He now switched to being sullen and said hardly a word until they drove up before her front door.

He switched off the ignition and sat moodily studying her in the shadowed front seat of the car. "I don't blame it all on him," he said. "You could have prevented what happened."

"I keep telling you it wasn't important," she protested.

"You could have shown some discretion," Dick went on. "Humiliating me before my friends. Letting him kiss you in plain view of the ballroom."

"No one saw us but you."

"So you think!"

"I'm positive of it," she insisted. "and anyway I don't care!"

"That's more like it," he said, delighted to have won his point.

Grace looked across at him unhappily. "Dick, I don't want us to quarrel. It was an accident. It won't happen again. Can't you let it go at that?"

"To make it worse, I'm sure Barney and Gail caught on," he said. "I'm sure they were laughing at me."

"If they're such staunch friends of yours, they wouldn't be."

"They knew you'd gone off somewhere with that Geoff and I couldn't find you," he said. "I was hardly able to talk after I came back from seeing you in his arms. They noticed it."

"Barney is too anxious to curry favor from you to dare say anything," Grace told him. "And Gail is stupid. I don't care for either of them."

"You'd prefer someone like Geoff Bailey!" he sneered.

89

"I do," she said frankly. "Now let's forget all about this. Kiss me goodnight, Dick."

He turned to stare bleakly at the dashboard. "Sorry. I'm not in the mood," he said sullenly.

"I'm sorry, Dick," Grace told him, leaning close to him. "I truly am." And she kissed him gently on the cheek. "Will you be over tomorrow? Dad always likes to get in a game of tennis with you when it's fine on Sunday."

"I'll see," he said, still not looking at her.

"Goodnight, Dick," she said in a soft tone and then let herself out of the car.

Not until she was in her room did it strike Grace that Dick might not rest until he had told her father. If he did, she thought, she'd not be able to forgive him.

Sunday morning was warm and fine. She and her father went to the eleven o'clock service at the Episcopalian Church of St. Anne. Aunt Florence was there in an enormous wide-brimmed hat, fanning herself periodically with the prayer book during the sermon. Dick Browning and

90

his mother sat down front, and Grace thought he looked grim and strained. A glance in the direction of the Bailey family pew showed her that Mabel was there with her father and mother and newcomer cousin Geoff. Geoff caught her glance and smiled for her benefit.

She turned away blushing furiously and gave her austere parent a furtive side look to see if he'd noticed. His eyes were fixed sternly on the pulpit, so she breathed a sigh of relief. Then the sermon was suddenly over and the closing hymn sung and they filed out of the church. Her father shook hands with the Reverend Moore without any exchange of words; he did not believe in making a social affair of church going.

Aunt Florence had somewhat different ideas. After loudly congratulating the colorless Reverend Moore on an excellent sermon, she came hurrying to join them.

"Well, Adam," his sister said breathlessly as she caught up with them. "One would think you were running away from an evil influence rather than your only sister."

"Good morning, Flo," he said grimly.

"I see you're in your usual boisterous spirits."

"I'm anticipating having dinner with you and Grace," she said. "Has Marie gotten home yet?"

"She has not."

"Well, I've been worrying about her," Aunt Flo said with a toss of her wide-brimmed hat. "I'll see you at the house." And she left them to go to her car.

Grace's father said, "Let's get out of here," and propelled her quickly over to their own luxurious town car.

On the drive home, her father said, "I'll not be able to speak freely in front of Florence. So I'd better ask you now. What happened at the club last night?"

"Nothing much. Just an ordinary evening."

"Was that young Bailey there."

"Yes."

"I saw him in church this morning," Adam West said in his cold manner. "He's making all the right moves. Preparing to launch his campaign from the best possible position. It will take more than an appearance in the Bailey pew to make his business here respectable."

"He has the right to attend church," she reproached him.

"I'd be the last to deny that," her father observed dryly. "But I do question his motives."

By this time they had reached the driveway and she was rescued from having to answer any more awkward questions about the previous night. She went in ahead to prepare for Aunt Florence. The old woman generally remained until mid-afternoon when Adam West went out for his game of tennis on their private court. Then she went home in her car for what she termed her 'beauty nap.'

Dinner was enlivened by Aunt Florence suddenly asking Adam West, "What about this strike at the plant, Adam?"

Grace's father looked as if he might choke. He waited a moment and then in too controlled a voice told his sister, "It need not concern you, Florence."

Aunt Flo's sharp, withered features registered annoyance. "Need I remind you I happen to be a principal shareholder of the company?"

He shook his head. "No. You do that constantly."

"So what concerns the company does concern me," the old woman said firmly. "Who is this Bailey person who has come here about a union?"

"A cousin of Mabel's," Grace said.

Aunt Florence seemed impressed. "The Baileys are nice people."

"It won't amount to anything," Grace's father assured his older sister. "So don't worry yourself about it."

"I'm not worried," Aunt Flo declared. "Merely interested! When you get to my age and live alone, you have few things to spark your attention." She helped herself to an olive. "I think I might enjoy a well-concocted brawl between labor and management in Branton."

"Brawls are seldom well conducted," he said with one of his cold looks. "But don't count on there being any."

"We all have great confidence in you, Adam," Aunt Flo said demurely in a manner to suggest the opposite. From long practice she knew exactly how to annoy this younger brother. And it had apparently become one of her few remaining pleasures since she scarcely ever lost an opportunity to indulge in the little game.

By two-thirty Dick Browning had arrived in white shirt and shorts, ready for the tennis court. He looked in a morose state of mind still, but he smiled politely for Aunt Flo and entered into a pointless discussion of the weather with her.

Then the old woman left, and Dick and Adam West went out to the tennis court. Grace sat down with the Sunday paper for the first moment of relaxation she'd had since hurrying off to church with her father. She'd barely scanned the main news section and was looking through the social pages when Hilda Olsen came bustling into the room.

"You're wanted on the phone, Miss Grace," the housekeeper said.

"Oh?" Grace put down the paper. She took the phone call in the hallway, and it was Geoff Bailey on the line.

"Sorry I didn't get a chance to talk to you after church," he said. "It was one of the main reasons for my going."

"Indeed," she said with mock acidity.

"My dad was suspicious of your motives in being there."

"He's a rough customer," Geoff said. "No repercussions about last night?"

"Only a minor explosion," she said guardedly.

"I hoped that Dick might ask for his ring back."

"You did all you could to help it along," she said.

"I'm still unrepentent," he assured her. "So you've made your peace with him."

"Call it a temporary truce."

"Then there's some hope," Geoff said.

"I should think you'd be more concerned about your business here than my problems," she said.

"Everything in its place," Geoff told her. "I was hoping you might invite me over on this quiet Sunday afternoon."

"I said goodbye last night. Remember?"

"I didn't take you seriously," he said.

"You'd better. Dick is here now. He and Dad are having a game of tennis. He comes over every Sunday when it's fine. So you see we're really a happy family group."

"I'd be more impressed if you and

he were playing tennis. Strikes me he's mostly interested in your father's good will."

"Is that all," she asked politely.

"It's been good talking with you," Geoff told her.

"I'm glad you enjoyed it," she said. "Now I really must say goodbye again."

"I'll be keeping an eye out for you in Branton," he promised.

"I rarely go in town," she said.

"Well, make an exception now that you know I'm around," he said in his teasing fashion. "And don't forget! I think Browning is wrong for you on every count."

He hung up before she could make any reply. And she put the phone down with a forlorn smile on her pretty face. He somehow always seemed to manage the final word. She knew he was a brash young man who was slated to bring her nothing but trouble, yet she couldn't help liking him a good deal. He certainly wasn't stuffy. She wished she could say the same for Dick.

Usually when the two men returned from their tennis they were in the best of humors. But on this warm Sunday she at once sensed something different in Dick and her father.

Dick began with, "The committee of the local organization has formed what they call an educational group."

Adam West frowned. "What kind of educational group?"

"They've been studying the history of labor unions."

"What do they hope to accomplish by that?" her father demanded.

"I guess they want some background so they'll know what they're talking about when they put up an argument to join the national union."

"Their desire for betterment is to be congratulated," Grace's father said with a derisive expression on his patrician face.

"I see nothing wrong in it," she declared to both men.

Dick waited for her father to speak, and when he did not immediately make an answer, the young man turned to her with some uneasiness. "There's nothing wrong in it. But they're really only looking for an excuse to cause trouble. They're not truly interested in education."

"How do you know?" she asked.

Dick looked surprised. "Barney Wells said the ones heading the educational group are a lot of troublemakers."

"He probably decided that was what you wanted to hear," she said.

Her father gave her a sharp glance. "Why are you so suddenly defending these people? You know nothing about them or what they're up to."

"You've told me quite a lot," she reminded him.

"You wouldn't be allowing yourself to be swayed by personal friendships, I hope," her father said. "I know Geoff Bailey has a great deal of charm."

Grace felt trapped and angry. "And courage," she said in rebuttal. "I can't forget he saved my life yesterday."

Her father smiled thinly. "A hero and a champion of the underdog. Can you match that, Dick?"

Dick's broad young face flushed. The crew-cut young man held his head. Staring at the carpet, he said, "I don't think he'll measure up so well when the real showdown comes."

"I'm glad to hear you say that, Dick,"

Adam West said blandly. "I agree." And he drained the last of his drink.

"One other thing," Dick went on. "Barney said that Dr. Daniels was acting as education counselor for the group."

Adam West put his empty glass down hard.

"Ray Daniels!"

"Yes."

Grace's father nodded grimly. "I might have expected him to have a hand in something like this. His radicalism goes back a long time. I thought when we got him out of the school system we'd eliminated his influence. So now he's found another way."

She was shocked to hear the vindictiveness in her father's tone. "You can't be serious, Dad," she protested. "Dr. Daniels is a fine old man. A man of education. I'm sure he's only trying to be helpful."

"He's a Communist at heart," her father snapped. "He always has been. In the early thirties he carried a card. That was what helped finish him when he came before the board."

"Then you behaved cruelly," she shot back. "I've known Dr. Daniels as a friend since my school days. We're doing some reading together now. And I can promise you he hasn't tried to twist my mind into Red channels."

Adam West frowned at her. "I wonder. In view of your general attitude and what you've said here today."

She stared at him. "What have I said that was wrong?"

"If you're not aware of it I won't remind you," Adam West said coldly. He turned to Dick. "Thanks for the game, Dick. I'll be in my office early in the morning. I'd like you to get me a full report of the names and employment details of every member of this so-called educational group."

Dick stood up. "Yes, sir."

Adam West gave him a curt nod and left the room. She and Dick stood there in a tense silence for a moment. Then Dick came over to her. "Shall we go outside?" he asked. "I'll be driving home in a few minutes."

She nodded and they went out through the open French doors into the garden. When they were out there and safe from being heard by her father, she said, "I think you needn't have stressed that educational committee so much. And you certainly didn't have to mention Dr. Daniels."

Dick looked unhappy. "I was only trying to brief your father on what's going on."

She gave the young man in tennis whites an accusing glance. "I could wish you had some better authority than Barney Wells."

"Don't underestimate Barney," he warned her.

"I just don't like any of this," she said. "I believe the company is taking a wrong stand about the union. And none of you has the nerve to face up to Dad and tell him so."

Dick's face took on an annoyed expression. "I agreed with your father."

"That's your trouble," she said. "You always do."

Dick sighed. "I guess there's no point in us talking about this. We see it differently." He paused. "About last night. I've been thinking things over."

She was instantly alert. "Yes?"

The young man with the crew-cut

blushed. "Maybe I was too hard on you," he admitted. "I did spend too much time talking to Barney."

"Did you really?" she mocked him.

"Sure. But I had a good reason," he said. "Anyway that doesn't matter. The thing is that I agree with you. We'd better forget about it. Just consider it never happened."

"I'm agreeable," she said.

"You'll not be seeing Bailey again anyway."

"I don't imagine I will," she said carefully.

He offered her an uneasy smile. "So we all make mistakes. You know I love you, Grace. I guess I was too jealous to think straight last night."

"So it seemed."

"Well, no lasting harm done," he said. And he came close and touched his lips lightly to hers.

She gave him a mocking smile. "A Sunday kiss!" she said.

Dick smiled uneasily. "I'll have to be on my way," he told her.

It wasn't until she had watched him drive off that it struck her. The way he had talked and acted, the sheepish approach to a reconciliation. And the harsh manner in which her father had behaved after returning from the tennis court with him. He'd been in a bad humor in contrast with his usual jovial mood. It suddenly added up. And she stood there forlornly convinced that Dick had betrayed her in a most miserable fashion. He had, after all, told her father about his finding her in Geoff Bailey's arms last night.

6

IT rained on Tuesday, but Grace drove to Dr. Daniels' cottage to keep her reading appointment with him just the same. The old teacher had told her they could work in his library if the weather was bad. The events of the weekend had left her on edge, and she looked forward to a long talk with the veteran scholar.

She parked her car in front of the cedar-shingled cottage and rang the doorbell. It was several minutes before the old man hobbled out to open it.

"Sorry to take so long," he said. "But in this weather my joints are a special problem."

"It's I who should apologize for disturbing you on such an awful day," she said, taking off her wet coat.

"I've been anticipating your visit. I get very lonely these days."

When they were comfortably settled in the small den which served as his library, she said, "I've been making some discoveries about you."

The old man's eyes studied her from behind his rimless glasses. "I trust your Aunt Flo hasn't been telling some more tales out of school," he said.

"No. I heard this from another source. I understand you're acting as educational advisor for a group from my father's plant."

His kindly face showed pleasure. "Yes. It's been very rewarding. These men are eager to learn something about union history and unions."

She sighed. "I think I may fairly warn you without being disloyal to my father. I overheard a conversation between him and one of his executives. Your name was brought into it."

"I'm not surprised," Dr. Daniels said. "Your father has never been one of my admirers."

"Father took the stand that your advising the labor group amounts to near-communism. Of course I know this is ridiculous, but I feel you should know what his thinking is."

"I found out his opinion of me when

I was forcibly retired from my school position," the old teacher said wearily. "I don't blame him. It is not his fault that his views are narrow by my sights."

"I think you're too generous," she said. "I have no idea what Dad and the company are going to do. But I heard him asking for the names and records of the men who have been meeting with you."

The lined face under the thatch of white hair showed no particular emotion. Raising one of his twisted arthritic hands, the old man made a gesture of resignation. "I'm not upset by your news. I'm safely remote these days. I have nothing to be taken from me except my life, and in my state of health it is no precious possession. But I fear your father is in for a shock. The men are going to present him with a request for a proper union. And unless he meets them fairly, they will strike. It could be a long drawn-out battle, disastrous to the townspeople and to the plant."

"Geoff Bailey, the organizer, has been here for several days," she said, "but nothing seems to have happened."

"No demands have been presented yet. But work has been going on behind the scenes. The showdown will come before this week is out."

"Father thinks the organization the men have locally is enough."

"Of course," the old man said dryly, "and perhaps under him it is. But suppose new management took over the firm? These men have no bargaining group. They need one to protect themselves. Nothing short of affiliation with a national union will give them the funds and strength they need."

Grace asked, "Do you think the men will win out?"

"I do."

"Have you met Geoff Bailey?"

The old man nodded. "Yes. They brought him here for a meeting the other night. I'm greatly impressed with him. He knows both sides of the story. He was once in management himself. His father's firm went out of business and he became a union executive."

"Dad tells so many stories about unions," she said. "Of the corruption and the abuse in them. That's one of

108

the main reasons he doesn't want the company involved with them."

Dr. Daniels smiled. "There is little perfect in this world, if anything. But, for the most part, the various unions have brought justice to those who would otherwise never have gotten it."

She smiled. "I hope you hear nothing more about this. But I wanted to let you know what I'd discovered."

"And I appreciate it," the veteran scholar said.

"Let us give no more time to it. Today I'd like to read some of the *Epistles* of Seneca with you. It will make a pleasant change from Shakespeare, and he had much to say to us two thousand years after his death."

Grace frowned slightly. "I don't think I know Seneca or his work."

"A Roman aristocrat of the early Christian era," Dr. Daniels said. "He was one of Nero's advisors. And while that unhappy emperor listened to him he managed very well. But Seneca became disgusted with the corruption and double-dealing in high places and resigned his position. Later his enemies forced him to commit suicide since they feared his criticism and the possibility he might return to power."

As she listened to the old man's account of the long dead scholar, Grace was struck by the parallel between Dr. Daniel's life and that of the renowned Seneca. The circumstances were different, but the basic facts remained the same. A good man had been pressured from a position of authority to rust in obscurity. And when he attempted to pass on some of his knowledge, he was again regarded with suspicion and plotted against.

Dr. Daniels opened the small volume on his lap and began reading to her. She found it extremely interesting and the truths of two thousand years ago were still valid. When they came to the period of discussion, there was plenty for them to talk about.

"What fools these mortals be!" the old man said quoting Seneca. "Surely we can agree with that."

"And I think this one is so apt," Grace said, finding a paragraph on the opened page of the book he'd passed to her. And she read it aloud: "Men do not care how nobly they live, but only how long, although it is within the reach of every man to live nobly, but within no man's power to live long."

The old scholar smiled his approval. "It's a lesson we all could profit by," he said. "And how about, 'All art is but an imitation of nature'? Isn't that solid truth?"

"I had no knowledge of him until today," she confessed, "but some of these phrases have been repeated through the ages."

"We've all been made richer by Seneca's wisdom," Dr. Daniels agreed. "We can end our study of his work by considering this: 'We are mad, not only individually, but nationally. We check manslaughter and isolated murders; but what of war and the much vaunted crime of slaughtering whole peoples?' I think that is one of his most biting comments."

She smiled as she passed the book back to him. "I'm sure my father would find some way to connect this philosophy with the teachings of Karl Marx and brand Seneca as the earliest Communist."

"It's entirely possible," he laughed. "Those on the far right can spot the red menace where you and I are color blind."

"It's been wonderful talking with you again," Grace said, rising. "And please don't try to help me with my coat or see me out. I can manage very well on my own."

"Thank you, my dear," Dr. Daniels said. "I'm not too proud to admit I would appreciate not having to move from this chair. Will I see you next week?"

"Definitely," she said. "Same time?"

"Same time," he said with a smile on his worn face. "Perhaps the weather will be nicer and we can enjoy the warm garden again."

She left him feeling less tense. There was a hint of retreat from the world in their meetings. The objectivity of their reading gave her a fresh perspective, helped her to assess her problems at true value rather than as looming threats.

It was still raining hard and she drove straight home. When she parked her car, she saw there was a small truck in the area reserved for the house cars. She didn't recognize it but entered the house without much thought about it. To her surprise she met Joe Spear in the hallway. He was carrying a leather bag of medium size and he paused to give her a knowing grin.

"Figured I was sure to miss you," he said.

She didn't want to reveal her dislike of him, so she smiled with an effort. "I've been in town."

"Just finished fixing the stereo," Joe said.

"Thank you," she said politely, waiting for him to go on.

But he stayed to study her closely, wearing that wise smile. "Fixing that thing was quite a job," he informed her. "It had a couple of tubes gone and a whole burned-out section of wiring. If it had been any worse, we'd have had to shop it to the factory."

"I'm glad you managed so well," she said, still waiting for him to go.

"Sure, I did fine," he said in his bold fashion. "Call me anytime you need help."

"I'll remember," she said, maintaining a patient front she didn't feel.

The dark young man looked around him. "This is sure some classy place. But I guess you wouldn't notice it, having been brought up in the lap of luxury so to speak."

She knew it was wrong to condemn him. To think that he was sneering at them and begrudging them at the same time. But that was how his behavior struck her. She said, "Dad likes nice things."

"Sure he does," Joe spear agreed. "And he has the loot to buy them." He gave her another nod. "Be seeing you!" And he was on his way.

Grace gave a sigh of relief. There was something cheap and underhanded about the brilliant protege Dick insisted on sending up whenever they needed something repaired. There were few people she distrusted on sight, and Joe Spear was one of them. Yet, to be fair, she couldn't say anything against him except for his overbearing manner. She went into the living room and tested the stereo. It worked.

About an hour later, Dick called her from the factory. "Joe tells me he cured the stereo. Have you tried it?"

"Yes," she said. "It's fine now."

"Good! Joe is a smart guy."

"He is," she agreed without enthusiasm. "How are things down there?"

"No problems yet," he said. "Could be the calm before the storm though."

"I've been listening to the radio for some mention of the plant's labor troubles but there hasn't been a word," she told him.

"We've asked the local media not to give it any publicity," Dick said. "It would only make things worse."

"I suppose so," she agreed, awed by the power of her father's company in so casually giving orders to the local press, radio and television.

"I'll see you tomorrow night if nothing breaks," Dick promised her.

As it turned out, there was to be no date. A crisis shaped at the plant Wednesday morning. The union sent a committee to interview Adam West in his office. He promptly refused to listen to any of their suggestions and warned that he would not recognize a nationally affiliated union in the plant. The reaction was equally swift. The committee warned him the workers would go on strike on Thursday morning and stay out until he would negotiate with Geoff Bailey. So Grace sat home alone Wednesday night while Dick conferred with her father and the other executives at the plant.

On Thursday morning the strike began officially. The news media no longer felt bound to silence, and almost hourly reports were issued on the showdown that could bring financial disaster to Branton. Grace spent a lot of her time by one or the other radios in the big mansion.

Thursday afternoon Adam West came home early. Grace met him as he entered the house. She could see that he had suffered a good deal of strain from the trying hours at the plant. His face had a nasty purple tinge, and remembering his heart attack of a few years before, she began to worry.

"Nothing changed at the plant?" she asked him.

"No." He shook his head.

"Haven't you tried to find a common ground for negotiating?"

"I can't meet their request for an outside union," Adam West snapped. "There is nothing to negotiate."

"But that makes it seem so hopeless," she complained.

"Hopeless for them!" was his reply as he strode to his study.

She watched him with despair on her pretty face, not knowing that within a quarter-hour, Marie would arrive with Mike. It had to be on this day of problems that her errant sister would arrive.

There was no warning. But Hilda Olsen came running to her in the living room with the announcement, "Miss Marie has just driven up in a little red car. She has a young man with her!"

Grace groaned. "Today of all days! Let me meet them first," she said. "I'll tell Father later."

"If you say so, Miss Grace," the housekeeper said, showing she didn't favor the idea by a dubious expression on her round face.

Grace went quickly to the front door

and was there to greet Marie and her young man with open arms. Marie let out an ecstatic cry of joy and hugged and kissed her. Mike was just a trifle more restrained, although he did take Grace in his arms a moment and touched his lips to her cheek. She stood back and surveyed the two young people.

Marie didn't look too bad after all. She certainly wasn't the newspaper vaunted hippie with slovenly dress and flowers in her hair. She was wearing a belted, full-skirted yellow dress that ended well above the knees to dramatize the black stockings she had on. Her dark hair was sleaked back in a ribbon, and she seemd to radiate a sense of well-being.

"You look wonderful," was Grace's comment.

Marie laughed and gave the young man an adoring glance. "What do you think about Mike?"

Grace turned her attention to the slim young man with his longish hair and sideburns. He had no beard to decorate his intelligent, pleasant face and he wore blue jeans and a dark turtleneck sweater.

She said. "I think he looks ordinary and normal."

It was the young man's turn to burst into easy laughter. "Right on both counts," he said, putting his arm around Marie.

"I suppose Dad is at the plant," Marie said, as they came inside with Grace.

She turned to warn them. "Not today," she said. "He came home early and he's in his study. There is some trouble at the plant."

Maried looked worried. "What sort of trouble?"

"A strike."

Marie gasped. "A strike in Branton? I never thought to see the day!"

"What about that?" Mike Blair asked. "We've landed right on top of the excitement."

"Not what I'd call the best moment," Grace said with a forlorn smile. "But I'm sure Dad will be glad to see you both." She knew in Mike's case this was a gross untruth but she wanted to make them feel as good as she could.

Before she could take them in to see her father, he appeared in the hallway.

119

Apparently he'd heard their voices and had come to investigate for himself. His lined patrician face took on a melancholy smile as he came forward to greet his youngest daughter.

"Marie!" he cried and took her in his arms.

It took a few moments for the excitement of the reunion to settle and for Adam West to be introduced to Mike Blair. His austere countenance showed pain as he shook hands with the young man. They went into the living room where Grace and her sister seated themselves on a divan with Mike standing uneasily by.

Adam West faced them with his shoulders back, his hands clasped behind him, and a stern look on his face. "The real joy I know in your return does not mitigate the fact you ran away from home, Marie," he said accusingly.

"I know, Dad," she said, looking down. "I'm sorry."

"It's quite easy to say that now," he told her. "But I doubt that you realize the mental suffering you caused me, your sister, and Aunt Flo. You behaved in a thoughtless and cruel manner."

"I wrote you where I was," Marie reminded him.

"And told us of your bohemian existence," Adam West snapped, "and of your friendship with this young man."

Grace felt she ought to intervene. "Dad, I don't think we should go over all that at this time. The main thing is Marie is back!"

"Please!" He gave her a stern look not to interfere. And now he turned his attention to the obviously nervous Mike. He said, "About this young man."

Marie looked up at Mike and gave him her hand to hold. Then she told her father, "I love him very much, Dad."

"I find that touching," he said in a cold tone that denied it. "But I need some time to find out a few things about him."

"Ask me any questions you like," Mike said bravely, still clutching Marie's hand.

"For instance, what do you do for a living?" Adam West demanded.

"I haven't been working in the past few months," Mike admitted. "I've been

121

lining up an idea."

"I see," Adam said with deep sarcasm. "And, of course, my daughter's income would prove adequate to support both of you."

"Dad!" Marie cried, her girlish face suddenly aflame. "You shouldn't say such unfair things to Mike!"

Her father gave her a silent, scathing glance and asked Mike directly. "Well, young man, did you or didn't you live off my daughter?"

Mike swallowed hard and then very patiently said, "We pooled our resources. My share wasn't quite as large as hers. I admit that."

"I guess so," Adam West said with relish.

"But we don't set as much store on monetary things as you do," Mike went on. "I mean it seemed to us the main thing was the happiness Marie and I found together."

"He's right, Dad," Marie said. "I've never known such a wonderful time. Not here. Not anywhere!"

Her father nodded grimly. "And how do you propose to support my daughter if I withdraw her allowance as I intend doing?"

"I intend to start a workshop," Mike said. "I have an M.A. degree, you see."

"Really?" Grace was sure her father was shaken slightly by this news. Then he quickly recovered and snapped, "You haven't been putting it to much use!"

"I said I was lining up an idea," Mike told him. "And I have been."

"What sort of idea?" the older man demanded.

Mike sighed. "It's going to be hard to explain to you, sir."

Adam West lifted his chin. "I believe I have reasonably average intelligence. Go on please."

"Well," the young man said, "I intend to open a workshop and lecture course on anxiety and tension control. I'll just take small classes, and the fee will be a hundred dollars for seven days' training." he paused. "I have my own methods based on the *Tibetan Book of the Dead* and on the works of Carl Rogers, Frederick Perls, and Susan Sontag."

"Just what is the nature of this so-called course?" Adam West snapped.

"Well," Mike said, "I think that all human beings possess a divine potentiality. And that my principles will provide specific ways to help my students toward a new capacity for love, feeling, and the ability to create. It's a program to free the joys of the senses."

Adam West frowned. "Do you think anyone will fall for that rot?"

"Dad! Don't talk like that!" Marie reprimanded him. "Mike already has the backing of a New York university. They are going to feature the course as part of their curriculum."

Her father looked surprised and angry. "I'll believe that when it's an accomplished fact." He glared at Mike. "In the meantime I think you should leave here and find someplace else to live. And until you've proven yourself, I forbid your seeing my daughter."

"I can't go along with that, sir," Mike said quietly.

Grace felt the situation was getting completely out of hand, that there was a good chance Marie would solve things as she had once before by simply running off again. And she couldn't stand by and see this tragedy happen.

Rising, she went over beside her father. "I'm sure you don't really mean what you said just now," she told him.

Adam West's aristocratic features were wrathful. "I meant every word. This young man will have to convince me of his worth before he marries Marie!"

Now it was Marie who stood up with a strange expression on her face. "Dad, you haven't changed a bit, have you?"

"What do you mean?" he demanded.

"Still the heavy-handed father," she said ruefully. And she took a step nearer to Mike and pressed close to the worried-looking young man. "Well, it won't work with me anymore."

Grace gave her sister an appealing glance. "This has been a bad day for us all," she said. "Let's not try to settle anything until later when we've had a rest."

Marie shook her head and with a bitter smile said, "No. We'll settle this now. You say Mike can't marry me, Dad?"

"Not until I know more about him," Adam West said.

Marie continued to smile. "Well, I'm afraid you're just too late. Mike and I were married in New York a month ago."

Adam West looked as if he might collapse. "You were what?"

"We're married, sir. We intended to tell you," Mike said.

After a moment the older man said, "I see," in a husky voice.

"So there's really nothing you can do, is there, Dad?" Marie said in a tone as cold as his own.

"It seems not," he said absently.

Grace went over and kissed Marie again. "I'm happy for you, darling. Happy for you both."

Marie nodded. And turning to her father, she said, "Now, does Mike stay here or do I leave with my husband?"

Grace stared at her father and saw the bleak expression of defeat on his lined face. He stood there frowning and saying nothing for a long moment. The weight of the silence in the big room was almost unbearable. She knew the inner turmoil he must be suffering.

Until at last he said stiffly, "This is

your home. Of course, I want you both to stay here."

And then he turned and walked away from them abruptly, moving down the shadowed hallway with a slow step. Watching after him, Grace was struck with the idea that this defeat had come at the worst possible time. It was bound to embitter him further and make him even more unrelenting in his dealing with the problem of the strike.

7

IN the days that followed, Marie and Mike slipped into the pattern of the household. Adam West accepted his youngest daughter and new son-in-law with a cold gracefulness. But it was plain he carefully kept out of their way whenever he could. The strike at the plant gave him a suitable excuse for this, and much of his time was spent at his office. Marie and Mike tried hard to be unobtrusive and took to picnicking around the area and visiting Aunt Florence frequently. They often remained with the old woman for dinner since the evening meal was the one sure time Adam West could be counted on to return to the house.

Grace tried hard to make peace between them all, and it proved a wearing task. Yet she enjoyed Marie being back and wished she would stay at home. But this was not to be since Mike had soon to return to New York

128

university that was featuring his course. Grace had come to like her brother-in-law and appreciated his direct approach to everything. She felt Marie had made no mistake in her marriage.

Her days were also complicated by intensive practice for an Opening-of-the-Season Golf Tournament at Bar Harbor. Jamie, the dried-up, little pro at the club felt she'd lost some of her form and was giving her an intensive polishing before she entered the contest at the adjacent summer resort.

The little man would shake his head and say, "You would'na wish to start the season with a defeat. Buckle down, lass."

She often paused in her stance to give him a rueful smile. "I'm doing my best, Jamie."

"Nae as guid as your best last season," was his doleful comment. "Get more ease in your swing."

And so it went on, day after day. It was gruelling work under the hot sun and she would return home at noon thoroughly tired out. Meanwhile the day of the tournament drew nearer.

Her father openly made caustic remarks about her preoccupation with golf during the crisis at the plant.

At home her attempts to communicate with her father all too often ended in a deadlock these days. She blamed some of his associates at the plant almost as much as she did him. They were too willing to cater to him and had made him expect to have his own way in everything. She pointed this out to Dick Browning when they were returning from a drive-in theatre on one of their infrequent dates.

Seated beside him in his car, Grace said, "How long do you think the strike can last?"

He kept his eyes on the road ahead. "I thought a few days would see it end. But now it doesn't look so good. Bailey is bringing in cash from the national union to make up payrolls for the strikers. They have no backlog of their own in the local organization. But with this outside help they can make it tough for the company."

"In other words, Bailey has come up with an ace," she said. "You counted on your employees giving up as soon as they missed their first week's pay. Now the whole picture is different. They've been given bargaining strength you hoped to deny them even before they affiliate with the national union. You can't hope to win, Dick. Why don't you make Father settle on the best terms he can make?"

"It'll cost us more now than it would have before," Dick said. "We'll have to try and outwait them. The national union is bound to have set a limit on how much they'll toss into this fight. If we can make them skip a few weeks of strike salary, the workers will get panicky and we may be able to dodge joining the big union after all. Or at least let them have membership on terms more favorable to us."

"I still say you're doomed to lose."

He gave her an annoyed glance. "Why do you insist on that?"

"I know Geoff Bailey. He's not the type to quit easily. And he isn't apt to enter a fight unless he has his strategy all planned. Father is simply wearing himself out and making his position more vulnerable."

Dick parked the car by the front

entrance of the house. Turning to her, he said, "You still seem to regard Bailey as some kind of hero. Have you seen him since that night of the dance?"

Grace gave him a teasing look. "Jealous?"

"I guess I have a right to be," the crew-cut Dick said stoutly.

"I haven't seen him," she said in a quiet voice. She didn't think it was necessary to let him know she and the union organizer had talked several times on the phone. And every time Geoff had tried to coax her to meet him.

"Bailey isn't your class of person," Dick went on. "He's no better than a lot of those union boss types. Your father was right to warn you against having anything to do with him."

"You told him, didn't you?" she said.

Dick's broad face showed confusion. "Told him what?"

"About finding Geoff and me on the club veranda kissing."

"Why do you say that?" he blustered.

"I can tell from the way you've acted since and the way Father has behaved toward me," she said. "What did you hope to gain by doing it?"

"You're just jumping to conclusions," he said without conviction.

"No," she said. "I'm sure of it. Were you afraid? Did you think Geoff would sweep me off my feet? So you reached out for Dad's help."

"I don't want to talk about it," Dick said.

She sighed. "It isn't a very pleasant subject, I agree. I really expected more of you, Dick."

"You know I'm crazy in love with you," he pleaded, reaching out for her.

"I suppose that's your excuse," she said resignedly. "I'll try to make myself believe you were justified." She eluded his arm to open the car door and get out.

Dick followed her up to the front door. "I'd like to see you more often," he said, "but I have practically no time of my own. I won't until the strike has been broken."

"I understand," she said.

He took her by the arms and studied her seriously. "I do love you, Grace. And things will be right for us when this trouble is over." And he kissed her goodnight.

Staring out into the darkness at the tail lights of his vanishing car, she came to the grim conclusion the illusion was at an end. And in a small voice she said aloud, "I'm not marrying anyone to provide a tennis partner for Dad or an executive with family ties to follow in his footsteps!" Having thus delivered herself of her convictions, Grace turned and was about to start upstairs, when the telephone in the hallway rang.

It gave her a start since it was well after midnight and few telephone calls ever came in at that time. Her first thought was it signalled trouble at the plant. Perhaps the strikers had started a fire or something equally as wild. So she hurried over to the phone and picked it up.

"Good evening," a male voice said pleasantly. It was Geoff Bailey on the line.

She gasped. "You! Why have you called here at this hour?"

"I passed you and Dick Browning on the main road," the young union man said. "You were too engrossed in each other to notice my car. I had an idea you'd be reaching home at just about this time."

"Well, you've proven your point," she said. "Goodnight!" And she was ready to put down the phone.

"Just a minute!" he pleaded. "I didn't call just to annoy you."

"That's what you've done," she said. "It's very late. If my dad wakes up, he'll be furious."

"I called you to ask you to have late coffee with me," Geoff went on. "I know a roadside place that's not far away and stays open until two."

"You have to be joking!" she exclaimed.

"I'm serious," he said. "We haven't seen each other for ages. I'm calling from a phone booth only a mile from your place. I'll be over there in three minutes. We can be on our way and back in an hour or so. And no one will ever know the difference but that you came in late from your date with Dick."

"Well," she said, taken aback. "You have it all neatly worked out!"

135

"Part of my training."

"And part of mine is never to accept after-midnight invitations from near-strangers," she said in a low voice, her eyes on the stairs as visions of her father appearing bothered her.

"There's something else," Geoff said. "I want to talk to you about the strike. I'd like to spare your father as much as I can. And you may be able to help. It's urgent I see you."

His pleading was earnest now, the bantering tone having vanished from his voice. She hesitated as she listened. Then she said, "You're not bluffing me?"

"Not in this," he said. "Give me an hour to talk to you. You won't be sorry."

She glanced at her wristwatch. It showed ten minutes to one. She said, "All right. I'll meet you if you promise to have me back here by two o'clock at the latest."

"You have my word," he said. "I'm on my way."

She quickly put down the phone and, drawing the sweater she'd worn over her dress about her, she slipped quietly outside again. The night was typically cool as she advanced down the several steps so she could meet Geoff in the driveway. She worried that she was making a mistake and that her father might wake up and raise a fuss. But it was too late now.

It couldn't have been more than five minutes at the most before Geoff's headlights came into sight. As she walked toward the car, it came to a quiet stop. When she got in and closed the door easily after her, she said. "I haven't any idea why I'm doing this."

The handsome Geoff smiled at her. "Put it down to my charm."

"No," she said. "It has to be more than that."

His eyes were fixed straight ahead as he speeded away from the house. "Let's say you really care for me."

"Not that either. It was your mention about the strike and Father. I hope it wasn't a cheap trick on your part."

"It wasn't," he assured her. "I've missed you. How have you managed to keep out of the way? You're never in Branton."

"I told you I don't go into town often," she said. "I've been busy at the club. I'm playing in a tournament in a few days."

"I see," he said. They were on the main highway now. "This place I'm taking you to isn't fancy. But it's quiet at this time of night. We can be sure of a minimum of privacy."

"It doesn't matter," she said. "Usually the small places have the best coffee."

"You won't complain about it here," he said. Soon he pulled the car in before a large diner with a metal front of white aluminium and a tall neon sign in red, blue and yellow that ran along the length of its roof announcing it was 'Jim's Highway Eat Spot.'

She laughed as they parked. "I guess I must have driven by here a few thousand times and yet I've never really noticed it before."

Geoff smiled. "Trust me to introduce you to the fancy places. What do you think of it?" he asked.

"Smells good! Diners generally do!"

"I'm glad you approve," he said.

She studied his handsome face closely.

"Now what was it you wanted to tell me about the strike?"

He furrowed his brows. "It's been going on too long."

"Isn't that your fault as much as Father's?"

"You know that isn't true," Geoff said. "I hoped when the committee sent in their recommendations your dad would act on them right away. They were fair enough. Instead he turned them down flat."

"He feels very strongly about this."

"So I gather," Geoff said dryly. "Now it's going to cost him more money. And today he had the fishing boats called in. The cold-storage facilities of the plant can't handle any fresh catches until the fish they have frozen there now have been processed. The plant is loaded with fish waited to be cooked and canned.

"And that means?"

"It means that the fishermen will have lost their revenue," Geoff said very seriously. "I can't offer any strike pay to the plant suppliers. They'll feel the pinch at once. And it's bound to make them angry. Probably will lead to violence."

"Or they could force the workers to a fast settlement," Grace suggested. "Don't you think Dad is counting on that?"

"It won't turn out that way as long as I feed the plant employees strike pay," he said grimly. "They may feel sorry for the fishermen, but they won't sacrifice everything for them."

"You think it may mean real trouble?"

"Strikes can be ugly when they get out of hand," Geoff warned her. "I've seen lives lost and property destroyed when it might have been saved. I don't want it to happen here. Isn't there anyone who can reason with your father?"

"Have you tried?"

"He refuses to give me a hearing. All the contacts are done through the committee."

The waiter brought them toast and coffee, and they remained silent until he left them. Then Grace said, "Of course Dad doesn't trust the committee. He calls them Communists. And he blames a local man, Dr. Daniels, for giving them some advice."

"I've met Dr. Daniels," Geoff said. "A fine old man. He's given a lot of his time to the boys heading the committee and they appreciate it."

"Dad can't think of anything but the fact Dr. Daniels had some Red affiliation away back in the dark ages."

"Communism was fashionable in those days," Geoff admitted. "I've had a few long talks with Dr. Daniels and he certainly doesn't hold Soviet views now. In fact, he was anti-Stalinist years ago from what he told me. And he's miles away from all that today."

"I agree," she said. "But I can't convince Dad."

"I'm sorry," Geoff said. "I was hoping you might intercede for me with your father. That through you I might get a private appointment with him at home. I think if I could talk to him personally I could convince him the union deal is just."

"I know it would only make things worse if I tried," she confessed. "He resents any kind of fixing. And that's how he would see this."

"But I do need to talk to him!"

She sipped her coffee. "Perhaps some opportunity may present itself," she said.

"I may have a chance to suggest his seeing you without having to drag it into the conversation. I'll watch for a chance."

"I guess I can't ask for more than that," Geoff admitted. "Only it had better happen soon. I can see the danger signs now. Something has to give before long."

Grace gave him a forlorn smile. "I've been on your side from the start. Yet I hate the idea of having to plead your cause with Dad. He's going to be very hurt. And he's not a happy man."

Geoff nodded. "I gather that."

"We'd better start back," she said, glancing at her wristwatch. "It's after one-thirty."

"There are a few minutes left," Geoff argued. "And we haven't spent any time talking about us."

"That wasn't why I met you."

"But I intended to bring it up."

She gave him an appealing look. "Please, Geoff! There isn't anything to discuss."

"You still plan to marry Dick?" he asked incredulously. "Knowing that you

142

aren't suited at all!"

"Why are you so bent on interfering?"

"Seeing you in the car with him tonight put me in a jealous rage," he was frank to admit.

She smiled. "But you hardly know me!"

"I disagree with you there. I'm in love with you."

"Geoff!"

"I mean it," he said earnestly. "And even when the strike is settled I can't leave Branton without some kind of understanding with you."

"You come here like a hurricane expecting to destroy everything," she told him. "Dick and I have all our plans made. We've been engaged a year."

"Isn't it lucky I came in time," he said quietly, "and made you face the truth. Because even if you won't admit it to me, I can promise you that you don't love him."

"We understand each other," she said, knowing this was also wrong but not wanting to give completely away to him. "We like the same way of life. We can be happy!"

143

"You never will!" Geoff said with brutal honesty. "It's my guess your father inveigled you into the engagement just as he's tried to rule everything else around here. The town is turning against him. Isn't it about time you woke up?"

She knew his condemnation of her father was right, and yet it angered her. She couldn't be put in the position of being disloyal to her parent. She loved him far too much and understood his personal unhappiness too well.

Her face pale, she rose quickly. "Take me home, Geoff."

He paid the bill and they left the diner. Little was said between them on the short drive home. But when he saw her to the door, he looked into her face with troubled eyes.

"I hope I haven't made you hate me," he said.

"You've made a good start," was her bitter comment.

"Please believe that I love you and want to help your father," he said. And he drew her to him for a meaningful kiss. Almost before it ended, she pushed him away and hurried inside. There were tears of bewilderment and unhappiness in her lovely eyes.

She was still in bed the following morning when the light knock came on her door. A moment later the door opened and it was Marie in night dress and robe.

Her younger sister smiled and said, "I knew it was too early for you to be up yet. Can I come in bed with you a minute?" It was an old custom between them, dating from their childhood days. Marie often snuggled into her bed at morning or night to exchange confidences and ask advice. Grace was touched that her sister remembered. She smiled and pulled back the bed clothes.

"Come along," she said. "But we won't have much time to chat. Jamie is expecting me at the club early."

Marie got into bed beside her with a sigh. "Jamie is a tyrant!"

"I know," she admitted. "But he's so set on my winning at Bar Harbor."

Marie gave her a knowing glance. "You were out very late last night. I heard you come in and then go out again."

Grace showed worry. "I hope no one else did."

"I don't think Father heard you if that's what you mean," Marie said.

"Dick and I went out to the drive-in first," she said.

"And?" Marie waited for her to go on.

She sighed, sitting up in bed, her hands clasped around her knees. "When I came back I had a call from Geoff Bailey."

"The union man!"

"Yes. I've met him several times. He's really very nice."

"Dad doesn't think so," Marie reminded her.

"And you know about Dad's opinions," Grace said, "and how unfair they can be."

"Don't I, though!" Marie said unhappily. "I'm sure he still hates poor Mike."

"Geoff talked to me about the strike. And then he brought me home."

Marie frowned. "What about the strike?"

"He wanted me to see if I could arrange a meeting between him and Dad before things really get violent."

"I see," Marie said. "Then there was nothing personal in all this at all?"

Grace smiled forlornly. "You wouldn't believe me if I said so."

"I don't think I would," Marie agreed. She looked away, out the window at the tall elm. "He claims he's in love with me. Says my engagement to Dick is a mistake."

Her sister didn't reply for a moment. Then she said, "How do you feel about it?"

"Just lately I've been disenchanted with Dick."

"But you agreed to marry him," Marie reminded her. "You must have at least thought you loved him!"

"Father managed it very nicely," Grace said with some bitterness. "I felt Dick was the right man. That we would learn to love each other. It hasn't happened, that's all!"

"Were you so aware of this before Geoff Bailey showed on the scene?"

She turned to Marie in surprise. "I'm not sure. I guess I was beginning to realize things were wrong in a vague sort of way. Then with the strike and

Geoff arriving I saw Dick in an entirely different light."

Marie looked worried. "I want to be helpful," she said. "And I never have been a fan of Dick's. But you've got to think this all out clearly."

"That won't be easy."

"I'm sure it won't," her younger sister agreed. "But you mustn't forget what Geoff Bailey might have to gain by winning your love. He could almost count on it having a favorable influence on the strike being settled. So it's natural he should try to turn you against Dick and Dad."

"He says he's in love with me," Grace faltered. "I guess I want to believe it."

Marie put an arm around her. "I hope he means it. But how can you be sure?"

It was a good question. But like so many good questions, it had no easy answer.

8

THE day of the Bar Harbor tournament was drawing near. Grace faithfully reported at the club every morning and was gradually winning the diminutive Jamie's cautious approval.

"The problem is to keep you at this level," he told her one morning as they came off the green.

She gave the little man an inquiring glance. "Then you think I'm ready?"

"Aye, I do that," Jamie said with one of his rare smiles creasing his thin weathered face.

Standing with him in the warm sunshine of the day in late June, Grace studied the distant green hills across the river. "That doesn't mean I'll win the trophy," she said.

"It gives you a sporting chance," Jamie said. "That's all we can ask."

Turning to him again, she said, "Dad is not pleased with my spending so much time getting ready for the tournament. He thinks it's not a serious enough occupation with the town upset by the plant strike."

Jamie looked disgusted. "Isn't he the one who's prolonging the strike?" he asked. "From what I hear, he's been unreasonable from the start."

She shrugged. "It's a nasty business. I wish it would end."

"Most everyone wishes that," Jamie said. "My brother-in-law's fishing boat has been idle more than a week now. And he has high expenses to meet and a family to look after."

"I know," she said. She could tell the little Scotsman was blaming her father for the strike as were most of the other people in town. In a way it was unfair. She knew he had tried to provide good working conditions for his employees and pay decent wages. He'd even encouraged their local organization. So he felt their attempt to line up with a national union was an act of ingratitude.

When she left the golf club, she drove into Branton rather than go home. She wanted to see just how the town was behaving under strike conditions. And she was surprised to note the main business district was extremely quiet. As she neared the end of the main street, Grace passed the brick building which had been occupied by a hardware store and recently vacated. There were now big posters in its windows announcing, 'Temporary Union Headquarters.' A cluster of grim-faced men stood by the entrance. She saw no sign of Geoff Bailey or anyone else she knew and decided he would likely be busy in the office inside or perhaps even down at the plant.

Leaving Main Street, she headed toward the waterfront and the rambling gray sheds that made up her father's fish-packing plant. Some of the buildings were several stories high, but a lot of them were one-storey structures extending out into the stretch of wharves that served the company. Here she saw men with signs picketing the various entrances to the many buildings. They went about their patrol quietly, but Grace could sense the tension in the air.

She had come to the last of the plant buildings and was about to take another street and start for home when she recognized Dick Browning standing on the sidewalk by his parked car, talking to the arrogant Joe Spear. Dick looked up and saw her almost at the same moment. So she had no choice but to brake her car and wait for him to cross over.

Dick's broad young face showed a smile. "We don't see you down this way often," he said, standing by the open window of her car.

"I was curious to see what was happening."

"Nothing much," he said, with a grim glance toward the plant buildings.

"I see Joe Spear is around," she observed, "and not in the picket line. Isn't he interested in the union?"

Dick shook his head. "Joe is smart. He's keeping out of it. If anything, he's on the management's side."

"I see," she said. "But then he is sort of a special assistant to you anyway."

"I guess you could call him that," Dick agreed. "How did your game go this morning?"

"Jamie seemed satisfied," she said.

"I may take a run down to Bar Harbor

and look at the tournament," he said. "If nothing flares up here and it seems safe to leave."

Grace was surprised. Dick had never shown any such keen interest in her tournament games before. She said, "That would be nice."

"I'll let you know," he promised.

"Perhaps the strike will end before the tournament," she suggested.

"I wouldn't count on that," Dick said. "In fact, your father is working on a plan now to bring in labor from the rural areas to operate the plant."

She frowned. "He shouldn't try that. Anyway, it isn't practical. You need a fair proportion of skilled workers."

"We think we can get a few of the key men to come back," Dick said. "It looks like our best hope of breaking the union."

"I think it's a dangerous idea," she said. "You should forget it and try to persuade Dad to talk directly with Geoff Bailey. I'm sure they'd come to an agreement."

Dick showed a nasty smile. "Your dad and I aren't supporters of Bailey, even if

153

you are. He'll never talk to him."

"You're not interested in a compromise, then?"

"No," Dick said. "The people of this town are beginning to see through Bailey and his game now. The fishing boats being laid up have caused a pinch. The strikers aren't too popular."

"I still say you're wrong," she said.

"Wait and see!" The crew-cut young man seemed very sure of himself.

She drove away with the feeling that Geoff Bailey hadn't exaggerated the situation. An ugly mood was growing in town. And Dick and her father seemed anxious to exploit it. This worried her more than anything else.

Hilda Olsen met her in the hallway when she got back to the house. "Your aunt called, Miss Grace," the housekeeper said. "In fact, she called you twice this morning. She wants you to phone her back."

"I will," Grace promised. "Where are Marie and her husband?"

"I don't know," Hilda Olsen said. "Miss Marie came out to the kitchen and made up a lunch for them and they

154

drove off somewhere."

"I see," Grace smiled. "Not likely they'll be back until evening then. I thought they might have gone to see Aunt Flo."

"I don't think so," Mrs. Olsen said.

Grace sat down and dialed her aunt's number. The old woman answered the phone herself. "It's you, Grace," she said. "I've been trying to get you."

"You should have tried the club," she said.

"I did," Aunt Flo told her, "but they said you'd just left."

"I went into town for a drive before I came home," she said. "I wanted to see what was happening at the plant."

"Things are coming to a pretty state," Aunt Florence mourned. "I wouldn't be surprised if there are battles in the street soon. That's why I've been calling. Dr. Daniels was struck by a rock this morning."

Grace gasped. "I don't believe it."

"It's true," Aunt Flo insisted. "It was on the radio."

"Did they say what happened?"

"According to what I heard," Aunt Flo

said, "he was sitting in his garden and someone threw a rock over the hedge at him. Later, the laundry man came by and found him unconscious on the flagstone path."

Grace was shocked. "That's awful!" she said. "How badly is he hurt?"

"Bad enough for him to be taken to the hospital. I wanted to let you know. You should go and see how he is."

"I will," she promised. "The poor old man! Who would do such a thing?"

"I don't know," Aunt Florence said bleakly. "They didn't give any more details on the radio. I've told you everything they said."

After promising Aunt Flo to get in touch with her later, Grace put down the phone and hurried out to her car. It was only a quarter-hour drive to the hospital. All the way there she was tormented by questions about the unhappy business. She knew that the veteran scholar was regarded with suspicion in some of the town circles, but she couldn't imagine anyone being so cruel as to deliberately try to hurt the near-crippled old man.

Branton Hospital was in the suburbs

at the other end of the town. It was a modern, red brick building of four stories. As the only large hospital in the area, it attracted patients from the entire country. Grace found an open place in the busy parking lot and, having looked after her car, hurried up the imposing granite steps to the hospital entrance. In the lobby she queried the information clerk as to Dr. Daniels' whereabouts and discovered he was in a private room on the second floor.

Grace walked up to the old man's room. His head was bandaged and his eyes were closed as if in sleep. She moved quietly to his bedside, not wanting to disturb him. But it turned out he was awake. As she stood looking down at him, his eyes opened. Recognizing her, a wan smile came to his lined face.

"Miss West!" he said. "I didn't expect to see you."

"I came as soon as I heard about your accident," she said.

"That was good of you," the old man said.

"Aunt Flo called me on the phone. I was out when she called first, but she left word for me to phone her back. She was anxious that I come to the hospital."

The veteran educator looked pleased. "Your aunt is a kind woman," he said.

"Have you any idea who did this?"

He sighed. "No. I'd just gone out to my chair. I heard a rustle from the hedge, and almost at the same instant the rock came whizzing at me. I was too surprised to attempt to dodge it. It hit me, and I tried to get up before I blacked out. They tell me they found me on the ground."

"What a mad cowardly thing for anyone to do," she said angrily.

"I've tried to search my mind for a reason for the attack," he said. "I can only guess it was someone who blames me for helping to bring about the strike."

"But that's so unfair!" she protested.

"I did give the committee some time," he was ready to admit. "But I made no positive suggestions for any action."

"Have you talked with the police?" she asked.

"They were here," he said with a touch of weariness in his tone. "They asked a lot of questions. But I wasn't able to tell them anything."

"Whoever did it should be punished."

He looked at her sadly. "I have no desire to cause trouble for anyone," he said. "It's probably some misinformed victim of the strike who's guilty. I guess the best thing is to forget and try to forgive."

"I don't agree," Grace said. "I want to see whoever did it caught."

"I appreciate how you feel," Dr. Daniels said. "You're young and you want to see every wrong righted. I'm afraid that isn't always how it works out."

"I blame my father," she said. "He's allowed this strike to drag on needlessly."

"He seems to feel he is in the right."

"And his yes-men rally around to encourage him," she said bitterly. "He won't listen to me or anyone who tells him the truth."

"Perhaps he'll have to learn the hard way," the old man suggested. "I hope not for the sake of the town."

"I'm going to tell him about you," she declared. "And I'm going to let him know I think you're in hospital as a direct result of his bad handling of the company's labor troubles."

"I warn you he won't agree with you," Dr. Daniels told her. "I think you might be well advised to say nothing."

"I'm sorry," she said. "My conscience won't allow me to do that."

"I wish you'd consider carefully," the old teacher said. "Conscience is not so much our master as we often claim. Remember what Montaigne said: 'The laws of conscience, which we pretend to be derived from nature, proceed from custom.' So keep that in mind."

"I'll let Aunt Flo know you're better," she said. "She seemed quite concerned about you."

"Thank her for me," he said.

She smiled. "You should be honored. There are very few people she bothers about. I had no idea you were good friends."

A smile creased the old teacher's face. "You could better call us old acquaintances," he said. "It's been years since we met. But, of course, we did grow up in Branton together."

"Aunt Flo is not one to forget," Grace said. "We'll all be worried about you until the strike is settled. You must be extra careful not to involve yourself again."

"I won't make any promises," Dr. Daniels warned her. "If the committee calls on me for information, I can't turn them away because I was struck by a stray rock. If this was done to intimidate me, they'll find it won't work. I've never been afraid to join an unpopular cause when I've felt it to be just. I'm too old to change now."

"You must think about your safety," she said.

"I'll cut down on my sessions in the garden," he promised. "I hope I'll soon be feeling well enough for us to resume our reading together."

"Whenever you like," she told him. And seeing that he was becoming tired, she left with a promise to be back another day.

The sight of the injuries he'd sustained had shaken Grace. And she headed home in her car determined to have a plain talk with her father. Never before had she felt so useless and frustrated. All her life she'd been dominated by Adam

West and allowed to do only what he approved. She wished fervently she'd had the spirit as Marie and run off as she did. At least Marie had found a new life and a husband who wasn't a rubber-stamp edition of her father.

She didn't see her dad until they met at the table in the spacious dining room. He gave her a cold glance as they sat down, he at the head of the table and she on his right.

"Mrs. Olsen says Marie and her husband are off picnicking again," he said.

"Of course you don't approve," she said quietly.

Adam West unfolded his napkin with great care. "I disapprove of many of the things they do. But it doesn't seem to worry them."

"I give them credit for that."

He looked startled. "What did you say?"

"I say I admire them for living their own lives as they think is right," she said. "I wish I could do the same."

His patrician face showed tinges of red at the cheekbones. "I have always tried to give you and Marie every advantage," he said.

"You have," she agreed. "But you have always denied us any freedom of choice."

He smiled coldly. "That sounds rather melodramatic," he said. "Surely this Geoff Bailey hasn't infected you with a lot of childish ideas along with kissing you on the club veranda in full view of everyone."

Grace stared at her father in silence for a moment. "I knew Dick told you," she said. "I was sure of it."

He shrugged carelessly as he buttered a hard roll. "Anyone who was there could have told me."

"No," she said. "It was Dick."

Adam West regarded her with curious eyes. "Why are you in such a state tonight?"

"I've just come from seeing Dr. Daniels in the hospital."

"Yes, I heard he had an accident," her father said in a disinterested tone.

"Someone injured him deliberately," she said with anger. "And it was probably done because he helped the strikers' committee."

"The town is disgusted with the strikers," Adam West said.

"You don't care do you?"

"It's not a problem of my making," he said firmly.

"You're ready to see others hurt without trying to stop this thing," she went on. "You're so smug in your own rightness and your stubborn wish to win!"

"I do not need you to lecture me on ethics," Adam West told her.

She could see that she had at least gotten through to him. So she went on. "I've spoken with Geoff Bailey," she said. "He made a personal plea that you see him. He asked me to talk to you about it."

"I can't say I approve of his tactics," her father said. "A pretty cheap trick trying to turn my daughter against me!"

"It's not he who is doing that," she said unhappily, "it's you. You're making me hate and distrust you. Just as you drove Marie away."

His eyes met hers. "Just how close are you and this Bailey?"

She hesitated. "We're friends."

164

"He's trying to use you, don't you see that?" her father demanded. "You have even less sense than Marie if you don't. He's turning your head with stories about his caring for you and trying to get you to intercede for him with me."

"Why won't you talk to him? Are you afraid?"

"I have nothing to say to that young man," Adam West snapped.

"So you're going on plotting to bring in outsiders to work in the plant and cause more people to be hurt," she said angrily. And she got up from the table in her rage. "Whatever happens, it should be blamed on you!"

"Thank you," her father said quietly.

Grace turned and raced out of the dining room and upstairs. When she was in the privacy of her own room she threw herself down on the bed and broke into loud sobs. The awful thing was that she loved her father, and yet he was destroying all the respect she'd had for him. How could he become so confused!

The tension at home increased. And feelings in Branton were running high.

She'd called Aunt Flo to make a report on Dr. Daniels, and the old woman had come out with some fresh news concerning the strike.

"Adam has imported some men from Bangor," she said. "They're starting work at the plant in the morning."

"I know he's planning something like that," she said.

"It will bring on a riot," Aunt Flo warned. "You see!"

"I see the danger but evidently he doesn't."

"Adam was always determined even when he was a little boy," Aunt Flo recalled. "But I expected that age would give him some judgement. It doesn't seem to have done so." And changing the subject, she said. "When is Ray Daniels going home?"

"He said he expected to be discharged from the hospital tomorrow," Grace said.

"I wish they'd keep him in there with all this happening," Aunt Flo worried. "At least he'd be safe."

"I agree," she said.

"And did you know Marie and Mike are returning to New York next

Thursday?" the old woman asked. "They're having dinner at my place Wednesday night before they go. Mike says that Adam makes him nervous. He stays away from the house as much as he can."

"Dad doesn't like him and he hasn't tried to conceal it."

Aung Flo sighed. "I can't think why. I say he's a nice young man. And he's calmed Marie down a lot. He's not the kind of person I expected at all. I did all that worrying about Marie for nothing!"

Grace gave a small laugh. "It should teach you a lesson."

"I want you to come next Wednesday night, too," Aunt Flo said. "No use inviting your father. He won't come, and if he did, he'd only make Mike uneasy."

"I'll be in touch as soon as I return from Bar Harbor," Grace promised.

"I almost forgot about the tournament," Aunt Flo said. "Good luck."

Marie and Mike did better than merely wish her luck. They went along in her car. She was glad to have their company and anxious to see as much of them as possible before they went away.

"I'm going to miss you," Grace confided from the wheel during the drive down.

They were both in the front seat with her as they followed the shore road to Bar Harbor. It was a pleasant day, and they passed through a number of quaint little fishing villages along the route. Marie, who sat in the middle, pointed out various places of interest to her husband.

Mike leaned forward to ask, "Why don't you pack up and leave with us, Grace?"

She smiled. "You forget. I'm an engaged girl."

Marie looked at her. "You're not really going to marry Dick, are you?"

"Perhaps. When all this trouble settles down. Only a little while ago we were making plans for building a house and deciding where we'd go on our honeymoon."

"He has more loyalty and consideration for Dad than he has for you," Marie told her. "I've been watching him since I've come home. He's worse than he ever was.

Mike has noticed it, too."

"I sure have," Mike said. "I'd call him a young man anxious to get to the top. And he's not going to cross your dad while he holds the power to put him there."

Grace kept her eyes fixed on the road. "You can't blame him for being ambitious," she said, determined to make what small argument in favor of Dick she could.

Marie sighed. "I just hate to think of you living on in Branton with both Dick and Dad ruling you."

She made no reply to this but instead changed the talk to the tournament. Mike was excited at the prospect of being on the sidelines as he'd never witnessed one before. They arrived in Bar Harbor before noon in plenty of time for the afternoon competition. By the time they had lunch, a crowd was gathering at the Bar Harbor Club, and Grace was scheduled to report for the all-important game.

Her adversary was a young woman from Portland. Grace, as defending champion, had the interest of the crowd from the beginning of the play. It was a strenuous game, and she began to wonder if she would justify Jamie's hard work to get her into shape.

In spite of the cooling breezes from the ocean the day was hot. And as Grace edged ahead first, then was overtaken by her opponent, and finally won the lead again, she felt the ordeal of the gruelling competitive event. She won by sinking a seven-foot birdie putt on the final hole. The girl from Portland congratulated her, and the local press photographers crowded around to picture the win.

As soon as she could Grace rejoined Mike and Marie. Marie's eyes were shining. "We're proud of you," she exclaimed.

"Great going," Mike agreed.

Grace was about to make a suitably modest reply when she was amazed to see Dick Browning separate himself from the crowd on the sidelines and come smiling toward her.

She ran to meet him. "You made it after all," she said.

Her fiancé nodded. "A little late. But I

hear you won. So a kiss of congratulations is in order."

Laughingly she accepted his kiss. "When did you arrive?" she asked.

The crew-cut Dick looked somewhat embarrassed. "I arrived in Bar Harbor at one o'clock," he confessed, "but I didn't come straight out here. I had to spend some time at the fish-packing plant on the other side of town. I'm doing some recruiting for our emergency crew."

Grace could only stare at him in silence, all the pleasure in his being there robbed from her. She could see through it easily now. He hadn't really come to attend the tournament. He was there on her father's business.

9

THEY all remained in Bar Harbor overnight. The local club had a dinner and dance in honor of the those participating in the tournament, and Grace and her guests were invited. She did not let Marie or Mike know that Dick had come to Bar Harbor primarily on plant business but let them assume, as she had at first, he'd wanted to be there to share her victory.

As a result, she noticed that Marie and her husband were more cordial to him than normally. She thought this was ironic but for the general good decided to keep the unhappy secret to herself. They had a table for four in the main dining room of the Bar Harbor Club and adjacent to the lounge where dancing was going on.

Dick seemed not in the best of moods, and Grace had an idea he would have preferred to go home to Branton rather than stay for the celebration. His mind was obviously back there as he barely carried his share of the talk.

Mike Blair was in a bouyant mood. The slender dark man advised Dick, "You should learn to relax, Fella. You've got yourself so tied in knots you can't have any fun."

Dick showed scorn. "What's wrong with being on the ball?"

"The eager beaver thing can be a hang-up," Mike said seriously. "There just isn't any final curtain. You keep on running even after you've forgotten what got you on the move in the first place."

Marie smiled at her husband. "Mike showed me the best way to enjoy life is to take it in a walk."

"That's the key," Mike maintained. "Life is a lot more fun if you pace it right. There are too many guys doing the running bit. What does it get them? Their names on the well-known executive doors and heart attacks at forty. And the way you're heading now, you're an A-1 contender, Dick."

"Thanks for your concern," Dick said with a sour smile on his broad young face. "So maybe I'd be better off with LSD, marijuana, and a guitar. You think hippies are due to take over?"

Mike offered him a good-natured smile. "After living in the East Village for five months, I'm willing to bet the flower people are on their way out."

Marie nodded. "I agree. A lot of them were deserting at the time we left."

Grace was quick to point out, "You two didn't actually live a true hippie life anyway."

"We were there to observe," Mike said, "and I picked up plenty. It will help me with my course."

Dick gave him a cynical glance. "You think your course is liable to pay?"

"It'll pay a lot of ways, man," Mike said seriously. "the enrolment is heavy and I hope to really help the people that come to me."

"Using the lore you picked up in the Village?" Dick said.

"That and a lot of other things," Mike told him. "Whatever you say about the hippies, give them credit for questioning the Establishment. They're not willing to take things for granted like you, Dick.

They're sensitive people who want to sort out the meaning of life."

Dick gave them all an annoyed look. "And I suppose I'm some kind of a thick-skinned hippo who doesn't know the score?"

"I wouldn't say that," Mike told him. "But admit it. You're deep in the Establishment bit. You are Daddy Adam's right-hand boy. And you're playing the game with him to the hilt."

Dick frowned. "Your father-in law," he said pointedly, "happens to be my superior. And I have respect for him even if you don't."

"Respect is one thing, man," Mike said. "Fawning is another."

Dick gave Grace an angry look. "Let's dance," he said abruptly and without waiting for her assent, he got up quickly and moved back her chair. Then he led her out onto the floor.

As they joined the crowd of dancing couples, he said, "I've had about all of that Mike I can take!"

"He's only trying to be friendly with you," she said.

"Friendly! He's spent the night insulting me."

Grace offered her irate fiancé a placating smile. "He's only been leveling with you, as he calls it. He's trying to get you to understand how he thinks."

"I know how he and all his scruffy crowd think," Dick fumed. "They shine at burning draft cards and joining protest marches. If we had to depend on them, the country would come to a dead halt."

"Maybe that would be good," she said. "It would give us all a chance to decide which way we're going."

"That doesn't sound like you, Grace," Dick said in angry surprise. "Are those two brainwashing you?"

"I think the world is less than perfect," she told him. "Even the world you and Dad represent. And I think it might be wise to think about what can be done and maybe experiment a little."

"I feel sorry for your father," Dick said. "Neither of you girls sees things the way he does."

"I certainly don't see any justice in the strike Dad has forced."

"His employees have forced," Dick corrected her.

"He's the one who refused to negotiate," she said as they continued dancing. "And now he's trying to hire a lot of strike-breakers. And you're helping him."

"It's my job," Dick protested.

"It would do you a lot more credit if you stopped agreeing with Dad on everything and gave him some real advice," Grace said. And she meant it.

The music ended, and Dick led her back to their table. Marie said, "You two looked wonderful on the floor."

Dick gave Mike a disgusted glare. "Well, of course, if Mike says so, I'm definitely in."

Marie's young professor husband took this in good humor. "I'm not the final word, Dick. But when you have my endorsement, you're on the way."

Dick glared at him. "Just what is this course of yours all about?"

"The joys of the senses," Mike said. "How to let them lead you to a new world. We begin with exercises. Then I have the students work in groups of six. They discover one another by touching in any way they find agreeable. Shake hands, embrace, touch a hand to the other's person's shoulder, just about anything to establish contact."

"Sounds crazy," Dick said.

"Wait until Mike explains," Grace told him.

"Right," Mike agreed, enthusiastic now that he was on his subject. "After a while these people begin to discover what they've been missing. They learn how their bodies feel under tension, grief, and fear. Instead of avoiding contacts with others, they begin to reach out. Other people are revealed to them and not as stereotypes. We pair the students off, not necessarily with a person of the opposite sex, and they talk about their problems and lose their inhibitions. By the time the course is over they are completely realized individuals."

"Sounds corny to me," Dick said coldly.

"I'm sure my father-in-law would agree with you," Mike said. "But I happen to think it's important to help people fulfill themselves. See them grow! I want to turn on the world."

Marie's eyes were bright. "And I want to help him."

The dimly lighted room was filled with the sound of friendly conversation with the dance music in the distance for a background. Grace felt that most people were having a good time, but she was definitely feeling the strain of keeping the two young men in a reasonable humor.

She finally said, "I don't think we should stay until the very end. We'll all be rising early to drive back in the morning."

Dick seemed delighted to have an excuse to say goodnight to the others. She left Marie and Mike to enjoy a final dance while Dick saw her back to her motel room.

She lay for quite a long while staring up into the darkness before she went to sleep. Aside from the satisfaction of winning the cup, the day had been a disaster from the first revealing moment when Dick had awkwardly admitted he hadn't really come to Bar Harbor to see her play until the prickly conversation with Mike. Once again Dick had shown up in a bad light.

Thinking this, it was only natural that her thoughts should shift to Geoff Bailey. The handsome young union organizer had made a definite impression on her. And in spite of the warnings she'd had from both her father and Marie, she had the feeling that Geoff had really fallen in love with her. But things were pretty hopeless since he and her father were on opposite sides of the fence. Any idea of a settlement between them seemed purely mad optimism.

Back in Branton the strike went on. Uneasiness grew in the town as Adam West put his pick-up crew to work. There were only enough men to operate part of the plant, but at least they had resumed production. Grace's father came home that first night after he'd managed this coup in a more genial frame of mind.

But Grace had carefully avoided congratulating him. She knew the scab workers would eventually bring the whole thing to a point of crisis. Aunt Flo shared her views along with a concern for the safety of Dr. Daniels. The old man was home again and he'd suggested that Grace come for her reading session in the evening rather than during the day.

"It would be better for me," he told her on the phone. "I'm working on some other material during the days."

So it was she arrived on Tuesday evening for her two hours' work with the veteran scholar. He received her in his small library and apologized for having her come in the evening. He had the bandage removed from his head, and there was only a small, livid scar to show where the rock had struck him.

"Have the police found out anything?" she asked.

Dr. Daniels smiled wearily. "I'm afraid not. I didn't expect they would."

"But they can't just drop the case!"

"I think it amounts to that," he said. "They've put it down to one of the fishing boat people."

"Do you agree?"

"No."

"Then you must have an idea who you think it was," Grace said.

"Only a hunch, my dear," the old man said. "And I'm afraid it wouldn't be counted as reliable evidence."

"But why would anyone do such a thing?"

"I've had two unsigned notes since I've returned from the hospital," the old man said. "They both accused me of planning the strike."

"Did you tell the police?" she wanted to know.

"Yes," he said, reaching out for a book with one of his twisted arthritic hands. "They didn't seem unduly surprised."

"I'd say it means the rock was thrown by the same party. Someone who blames you for his being out of work."

"I'd gather that," the old scholar agreed.

"It shouldn't be impossible to find out if the police really work at it," was her opinion.

"But then, as they explained, they have so many other duties."

"Maybe they're not anxious to find who it is," she said.

"I think they do want to avoid trouble," he agreed. And opening the book on his lap, he said, "Tonight let us spend some time with Thomas Carlyle. I have been doing some research in connection with his work lately, and so it fits in."

It was mostly a case of listening as the old scholar read aloud to her. She was happy to be inquiring into the great works of literature again with him to spark her mind to proper appreciation. The minutes rushed by and before she knew it they had come almost to the end of their two hours.

"I had no idea of the wide range of Carlyle's work," she admitted.

Dr. Daniels nodded and smiled. "Very few do. Some of his words have the true ring of greatness. Consider then: 'Nothing that was worthy in the past departs; no truth or goodness realized by man ever dies, or can die.' I find great comfort in that in these troubled days."

She said, "It's wonderful to be back at work with you again."

"I trust you're in no hurry," the old teacher said. "I was hoping you might be willing to brew me a pot of tea."

"I'll be glad to," she said, rising.

His eyes twinkled. "I like a cup of tea after work at night. But with my joints in the condition they are, I seldom take the trouble to get it. This will be a special treat, and you shall share it with me."

Darkness had come to the cottage during their reading and so she switched on the kitchen light when she went out to prepare tea. For a bachelor establishment she found the kitchen neat and well-kept. This was especially commendable when one considered that he was almost an invalid from his advanced arthritis. When she had the kettle on to boil, she went back to the library.

"Would you like something to eat with the tea?" she asked.

"There are some sugar cookies in a tin," he said. "I think they might be nice. One of my neighbors brought them in after I returned from the hospital." And he told her where to find the tin.

It was only a few minutes later that she brought in a tray with the teapot, cups, and a plate of cookies. As she put the tray on the table and prepared to pour his tea, she said, "I like being useful for a change."

"You lead a very busy life," he told her.

"Busy, but I wonder if it's all that useful." she said.

"You run your father's house."

She smiled as she handed him his cup. "Mrs. Olsen really does that. Oh, I look after the general details. But she carries them out."

"I'm sure your father would agree he needs you there."

"I wonder," she said. "He's accused me of wasting my time in the face of all the trouble at the plant."

Dr. Daniels placidly sipped his tea. "I can imagine the strike has made him irritable," he said.

"It's caused a wide rift between us," Grace said, sitting down with her cup of tea. "I don't think we'll ever be as close again."

"I wouldn't worry about that now," the old man said.

"When the strike ends, I'm going to have to face some personal decisions," she told him. "Among them, if golf and marriage to Dick Browning are going to be enough to fill my life."

Dr. Daniels' kindly face showed sympathy. "You have a fine mind. I wouldn't want to see it wasted."

She smiled. "I'm not that brilliant. I miss so many of the things in our reading unless you point them out for me. But I think even an ordinary life should have some direction and purpose. Winning regional golf tournaments could hardly come under the heading of dedication."

"You've been engaged to the Browning boy a year at least."

"Just about that."

"Then you must know him well by now," the old man said. "You must have some idea of the sort of husband he'll make."

"I have," she said. "And that's why I'm worried. It's not that he isn't practical and industrious. He's probably much more levelheaded than Mike. And yet I know Marie is tremendously happy in her marriage."

He eyed her perceptively. "I assume things have happened since the strike to worry you about Dick Browning. It's been a testing period for him."

"And it isn't that he's failed Dad," she was quick to point out. "He's stood right behind him. Done everything that Dad

186

could have wished. In fact, he's made himself a carbon copy of my father in so many ways it's frightened me."

"Well, at least you've come to know that," the old man said. "It's better than finding out after you're married."

Grace sighed. "The point is, can either of us change enough to make our marrying more than a mad gamble."

"Marriage almost always is a gamble."

"But when you know the odds are against you from the start?"

The old scholar nodded. "I say then you should give the matter some careful consideration."

"It's what I'm trying to do. Without much success, I may add. I know Father would be furious if I broke my engagement with Dick."

"I imagine so," Dr. Daniels agreed. "He's bound to see the young man as perfection since he's so much like himself."

She laughed. "I wish Dad or Dick had your sense of humor. They're both so deadly serious about everything."

"Your father had a strict bringing up," the old teacher told her, "and losing your mother was a bad blow. I think he retreated into himself then and, except for his business and you girls, he's shown little interest in anything since that time."

"Even Aunt Flo is less austere," Grace said.

The old man's eyes twinkled. "I can remember a day when your Aunt Florence wasn't austere at all. She was a tall, truly lovely young woman who charmed most of the men in this county."

"And yet she never married!"

"That was a tragedy," Dr. Daniels said. "A stupid tragedy."

"Do you know why?"

"I'm not sure," he said. "I think I do. Perhaps one day I'll feel certain enough to tell you all the details."

"She takes a great interest in you," Grace said. "You must be about the same age. I wonder you aren't closer friends. That you don't see each other occasionally."

The lined old face showed a smile. "We send each other cards at Christmas. It's always a comfort for one to know the other is still around. I'm afraid there's not much left beyond that."

"Would you like some more tea?" she asked, lifting the pot.

He held out his cup and again she noticed the swollen distortion of his hand. "Just about half-full," he said. And when she had poured in the right amount, he sat back with a relaxed sigh. "It's good to have this talk."

"It's been very good for me," she confessed. "Except that I have no right to burden you with my problems."

"I like to consider myself your friend," Dr. Daniels told her. "Surely I have a right as a friend to try and help you."

"You have."

He stared at her over his cup of tea. "You've talked a lot about Dick," he said. "But you haven't told me if there is anyone else."

"I'm not sure if there is."

"Yet, you don't sound positive."

"It's someone I really don't know well," she admitted, "and yet someone I've come to like and respect a great deal."

"Oh?" the old man lifted his eyebrows.

"Geoff Bailey, the union man."

Dr. Daniels didn't look surprised. "I'm not as removed from the happenings here as you might guess," he said. "And I've had an idea there might be something between you and that young man."

She felt her cheeks warm. "You couldn't have known."

His eyes twinkled. "Suppose we say I had some information from another party."

"But who could tell you?"

"Geoff himself. He's been here quite a few times," the old man reminded her. "And on several evenings when we've been here alone talking, he brought up your name. Very discreetly, of course. But he has had you on his mind."

Grace made no attempt to hide her pleasure. "I've done some thinking about him," she admitted.

"He's a fine young man."

She gave Dr. Daniels a significant look. "But I've also been warned against him."

He frowned. "Warned? In what way?"

"My father thinks Geoff is only pretending friendship with me to get to him. And Dick says much the same thing.

You see, up until now, Dad has refused to meet with Geoff personally. And he asked me to try and arrange a meeting."

"He might have done that anyway. Why should you suspect him of an ulterior motive for professing that he likes you?"

"I don't," she said. "They do."

"Then I'd say they are wrong," Dr. Daniels told her. He paused to glance at his pocket watch, a heavy gold one which he removed from a vest pocket. "I had a nice surprise for you tonight," he said, returning his watch to his vest again. "But I'm afraid it isn't going to turn out as I'd hoped."

"Oh?" she said.

"When I asked you to remain and prepare some tea, I expected Geoff Bailey would join us. But it seems something must have detained him."

"I would like to see him," she confessed. "We haven't met since I returned from Bar Harbor."

"The pressures of the strike have been growing," Dr. Daniels said. "His problems have increased in the last week."

She smiled. "Anyway it was a nice thought."

"We'll arrange for it another time," the old teacher said. "And I wouldn't make any rash decisions if I were you."

"I won't," she promised.

She was about to take the tea things out and wash up when there was the sound of a car drawing up out front. She and the old man exchanged knowing glances. A car door opened and shut and then there were footsteps on the gravel path and the front doorbell rang.

Dr. Daniels smiled at her. "That must be him. Will you get it?"

With an almost uncontrollable excitement she hurried out to the door and opened it. It was Geoff in a light suit and wearing no hat. He looked rather tired but smiled when he saw her.

"Unexpected surprise!" he exclaimed happily. And since they were hidden by the hallway from Dr. Daniels in the library, he bent close to kiss her. "I suppose the doctor has given me up."

"He thought you might be busy," she said.

"I was," he told her as he followed

her along the hall to the room where the old man was waiting. When he entered the small library, he went forward and shook hands with Dr. Daniels. "Forgive my lateness," he said. "But we had a fire at union headquarters tonight."

10

"**A** FIRE," Dr. Daniels said. "How did it start?"

"In some trash in the basement of the building," Geoff said. "There was a store in there before us. They left a lot of cardboard garbage behind. Somebody deliberately set it afire."

"Oh, no!" Grace gasped.

"I'm afraid so," the young union man said grimly. "There was no other way it could have started. None of us went down there."

Dr. Daniels showed concern. "Was there much damage done?"

"Not too much," Geoff said. "We could have lost a lot of valuable papers. Mostly it turned out to be a nuisance. The smoke drove us all out of the building."

"No wonder you were late," Grace said. "Have you any idea who might have done it?"

Geoff's handsome face showed uncertainty. "It had to be someone

194

opposed to the union."

"One of the fishermen, perhaps," the old man in the chair suggested, "or somebody at the plant who isn't in favor of the union."

Grace felt she ought to make some comment on this. She said, "I'm sure my dad didn't know about it. He wouldn't sanction anything of that sort."

Dr. Daniels made a positive suggestion. "Join us in some tea. I'm sure Grace has plenty left in the pot."

Geoff gave a faint smile. "I'm just about ready for something like that," he said.

She checked the teapot and discovered there were at least two or three cups left. Finding a third cup and saucer, she gave it to Geoff and poured out his tea. "If it's not warm enough, I'll make a fresh pot."

He eyed the teacup and smiled at her. "It's strong, and that's the most important thing." And he took a chair across from the veteran teacher.

"You may be wrong about the fire," Dr. Daniels said. "Sometimes waste of that kind goes up in flame without any outside factor."

195

The young man shook his head. "I don't think so in this case, sir. The rear cellar door had been forced open. Someone had been in there."

There was a sigh from the old man. "Too bad," he said. "It could be all that's needed to encourage more violence."

"I've warned our people that's no solution," Geoff said. "There's nothing else I can do."

"When Dad hears about it, he'll be furious," Grace said. "Even though I know he wants to defeat your union plan, I'm certain he wants to do it fairly."

"This is the second incident to my way of thinking," Geoff told her as he took a drink of his tea.

"The second?" she said.

"Yes." He glanced at Dr. Daniels. "I'd say the attack on you was the first."

The old man raised a swollen hand in protest. "I wouldn't decide that too quickly," he said. "I was the victim of some child or at the worst a misguided crank. I wouldn't blame anyone mixed up in the union battle."

"I disagree," Geoff said. "Everyone knew you were advising our educational committee. That rock was thrown as a warning and a punishment. The violence has all been on the other side."

Remembering how her dad hated Dr. Daniels, Grace found herself feeling ill. All at once it seemed possible that he might be aware of what was going on. She fervently hoped not. But she couldn't be as sure as she'd been before the news of the fire.

Geoff shrugged. "I have to try and avoid any continued trouble. This is becoming one of my worst assignments."

The old man gave her a look and with twinkling eyes told Geoff, "Yet I hope you don't consider your coming to Branton a complete loss."

"Definitely not, sir," Geoff replied courteously. "If only because of meeting you and Grace."

"I'll agree with you about Grace at any rate," Dr. Daniels chuckled. "And doesn't she make excellent tea?"

"The best," Geoff said, placing his empty cup on a side table near him. "And now I must be going. I came only to explain. I realized it was too late to stay."

"No need to rush off," the old man said.

"I must really go, too," Grace said rising. "It's getting late."

Geoff was on his feet with a smile. "I'll see you to your car," he said, "and then I'll go back to headquarters. Some of my people are still there."

They took the tea things out into the kitchen and said their goodnights. Then Geoff escorted her out into the refreshing night air. There were myriads of stars in the sky and the perfume of summer hovered over the darkness.

"It's so lovely tonight," she said as they reached her car. "Why do people have to spoil things?"

"Perversity of the human," he said, his handsome face showing a bitter smile. "I've missed you."

"And I've thought about you," she said quietly.

He suddenly looked worried. "Grace, no matter what happens, I don't want you to let it come between us."

His words struck a cold chill in her.

"Why should anything happen?"

"After the fire tonight I'm ready for trouble," he warned. "And it could be worse before it improves."

"You said there'd be no reprisal." she reminded him.

"But suppose we're hit again and some hot head takes it on himself to even the score?" he demanded. "You see how one thing leads to another."

"I think the important thing is that we have faith in each other," she said.

"Of course you're right," he agreed. "It's strange that one man should hold the key to the whole situation here and he should be your father. I'd allow myself the luxury of hating him if it weren't for you. Did you ever have a chance to talk to him about seeing me?"

"I tried," she said. "It didn't work out."

"I hardly expected it to," he said. "I've never met anyone so unreasonable. At least in other places I've always been given a hearing."

"He may still change his mind," she suggested. "Perhaps when he hears about the fire it will make a difference."

Geoff shook his head. "Don't count on it." He paused. "When will I see you again?"

"I don't know. It's awkward with feelings in town running so high."

As she finished speaking, a car came down the street and for a minute its headlights caught her and Geoff Bailey full in their beam. They had a blinding effect in their brief moment of passing and, as the car moved along, they were left in the shadows again.

"He said, "I'll phone you. That's the best way."

"Probably so," she agreed.

"This is something I can't do by phone," he told her with a sad smile as he gently put his arms around her and held her close while his lips caressed hers.

As they parted, she said. "Oh, Geoff, I'm frightened!"

"Frightened?" he still held her loosely.

"Yes," she looked up at him with troubled eyes. "Frightened for you and for Dad. I think you're right. Something awful is going to happen!"

"I talked too much," he said lightly. "Don't believe it. Maybe Dr. Daniels was right after all. The fire may have started by itself."

"You said someone had broken in!"

"Did I? You mustn't worry about it," he told her.

But worry about it she did. All during the lonely drive home she went over the events of the evening in her mind. She felt they had played a large part in building the apprehensions she felt now. The warm summer night had an ominous silence that terrified her. At any moment she felt the evil might begin.

She was filled with these fears when she went inside. And she was not prepared to see her father.

"You are very late," he said coldly.

She swallowed hard. "I was at Dr. Daniels for my book study," she said.

"You told me where you were going before you left," he reminded her.

"We read later than we intended. And I made some tea. It was late before we realized it."

Her father's patrician face bore a strange expression. "You apparently find great pleasure in the doctor's company," he observed in his acid way.

"He is an interesting old man."

"Indeed," Adam West said with heavy sarcasm. "And what about the young man who was there?"

"Young man?" she questioned, stalling for time.

"Don't lie to me," he snapped. "I know you met that Geoff Bailey there."

"What of it?"

"After I'd expressly forbidden you to have anything to do with him!"

"He was Dr. Daniels' guest," she pointed out. "I had no part in his being invited there."

"You'd like me to believe that, wouldn't you?"

"It's the truth!" she insisted.

"It would be closer to the truth to say it was an assignation arranged between you two."

"It was no such thing!"

"Brought about by Dr. Daniels' connivance," he continued angrily as he took another step down toward her.

"We came at different times," she said. "He only was there a little while."

"And you left together!"

202

Her eyes opened wide. "How do you know that?"

"Because I was told," he said triumphantly. "I have a witness who saw you standing together outside the house."

As she listened with growing disbelief, she suddenly recalled the car. The car that had roared by to spotlight them in its headlights briefly. But long enough for them to be seen. And whoever it had been had not lost any time in reporting them to her father.

"What a miserable trick!" she stormed. "To have people spying on us."

"I have no choice," her father said. "Otherwise you'd lie and cheat."

"And I suppose you had no choice about that stone that was thrown at Dr. Daniels or the threatening letters written him. No choice about having someone start that fire at the union headquarters tonight."

Her spirited attack on him must have come as a blow. "I had nothing to do with that fire," he said.

"I wonder!" Her tone was bitter.

"So Bailey is filling you with propaganda

while he tells you he's in love with you. It's about what I expected!"

"You're to blame for all that's happening," she scolded him. "Why don't you meet Geoff and settle the strike!"

"He'd like that now that things are going against him," Adam West said with a hard smile.

"Dad! What's wrong with you?" she begged, her eyes moist with tears.

"I could well ask you the same thing," he said.

"We've never disagreed like this before!"

"There was no Geoff Bailey to come between us," he said. "You've let this outsider turn your head!"

"That's not true, Dad!"

"It's evident in everything you say! Everything you do!"

"How can I prove you are wrong?" she begged.

"That would be quite impossible," he said coldly. "I'll only ask you not to betray me with that young man again."

"Is that all you came down here to tell me." she said with shocked resignation."

"Yes."

"Very well, Father," she said with a new humility. "Thank you." And quickly brushing past him she ran upstairs so he wouldn't see her tears.

Her unhappy mood continued on the next morning. It was apparent enough to catch Mike's attention. He came to her where she was reading in the garden and giving her a teasing glance, said. "What's wrong? You look like a kitten of doom!"

She glanced up at her brother-in-law with an embarrassed smile. "Sorry. I didn't intend to."

"Things going badly with Dick again?" he asked.

"Not really. It's just the tense atmosphere that upsets me," she said. "You and Marie are the lucky ones to be leaving."

"I'd say so," Mike told her. "But she doesn't like to go with things so confused. She's especially worried about you."

"I'll manage," she said.

"Your Dad can be pretty tough," he warned her.

She sighed and folded the newspaper she'd been reading. "Then maybe I'd better toughen up as well."

"It would be wise," Mike said soberly.

"I've always let Dad lead the way," she went on. "And I've followed his advice up to now. But I'm going to have to borrow from your hippie friends. I need their questioning technique."

He nodded enthusiastically. "That's the idea!"

"Give me a little time," she said.

"And what about this Dick? You know he's a square without a thought of being anything else."

"You two don't have the right chemistry for friendship," she said with a wary smile.

"I don't dig Dick or his general type," Mike admitted, squatting down on the ground beside her and absently picking up a long stem of grass to crinkle in his fingers.

"That was plain enough at Bar Harbor."

"Stay clear of him, Grace," her brother-in-law advised. "You'd be happier being like Aunt Florence and not marrying at all."

She laughed forlornly. "I'll keep that in mind."

Mike and Marie went off on one of their excursions after lunch leaving her alone. She waited around, hoping the phone would ring with some good news from Geoff, but there were no calls. So she drove by her aunt Flo's and found the old woman on the rear veranda enjoying the air and a view of the river. She gave Grace a sharp appraisal with her faded blue eyes. "What's happened to you?" she asked. "You look as glum as a January crow!"

"I feel it," Grace said, smiling ruefully as she sat down.

"What's wrong now?"

"A lot of things," she said. And for the first time she told the thin, imperious old woman all the details of her problem. Of her sudden turning against Dick and her love for Geoff Bailey. And of her worry that some calamity would grow out of the strike to ruin her romance with the young man. Aunt Flo heard it all without a change of expression on her lined face.

When Grace had finished, Aunt Florence eyed her with grim satisfaction. "I was certain something like this would happen," she said. "When Marie came back with such a presentable husband, I knew it would stir a rebellion in you!"

She looked surprised. "I don't think that had anything to do with it!"

"But of course it did!" Aunt Flo said with a toss of her head, the gray-blue hair vivid in the bright sunshine. "And then Adam has to handle everything in exactly the wrong way!"

"Why must he be so stubborn?"

"I asked myself that question first nearly fifty years ago," she said. "Adam was unforgiving from his cradle days. So he has no surprises for me now."

Grace gave her Aunt an appealing look. "Aunt Flo what am I to do?"

"Don't marry the wrong man whatever happens," the old woman warned.

"I don't want to hurt Dick," she said.

"The worst harm you could do him would be to marry him when you don't love him."

"I doubt if he'd mind that. We discussed it when we were first engaged, and it was his opinion that we'd learn to love each other."

"Poppycock!" Aunt Flo said indignantly. "You know your feelings for this Bailey are quite different from anything you ever felt for Dick. You can't fool your heart!"

"But I owe some loyalty to Dad," she worried.

"Loyalty and love are often in opposite camps," Aunt Florence warned her. The old woman sat back in her chair with a bleak expression on her thin face. "It is better not to weigh them against one another. I tried it and failed miserably."

"You?" Grace studied her aunt with astonishment.

She nodded. "Yes. Haven't you ever wondered about me and Ray Daniels?"

"I have lately," Grace admitted. "You both seem so concerned about each other and yet you never meet."

"That's because I made a foolish mistake many years ago," Aunt Flo said. "I was presented with a situation something like the one you are facing now. Ray asked me to marry him, but my father didn't approve."

"You were actually going to marry Dr. Daniels?"

"Yes. And I should have. But just when we were ready to set the date, I found out he'd been active in a Communist group. My father discovered it and asked me what I was going to do. I buckled down to his wishes and called the marriage off."

"But that seems ridiculous!" Grace protested.

"It does now," Aunt Flo agreed. "But this happened years ago when the idea of a radical marrying a West couldn't be countenanced. I suppose that's why I take so much delight in Marie marrying Mike."

"And all these years you and Dr. Daniels have gone on living in Branton. Not seeing each other."

"I blame myself that he remained here," the old woman said. "He could have done so much better somewhere else. And all his career he's had to fight that Red taint. It ended when Adam used Ray's arthritis as an excuse to retire him early from the post of high-school prinicpal. Adam's real reason was he felt Ray was emphasizing the new freedom of thought too much."

"How could Dad be so vindictive?"

Aunt Flo smiled wearily. "He's a true West. My father was just as proud and unrelenting. So you'll have to learn how to protect yourself against him."

Grace considered this thoughtfully. "Mike told me the same thing," she said.

"Mike is a smart boy," Aunt Flo said with enthusiasm. "I'm sure he and Marie are going to do well. They're coming here tomorrow night for a farewell dinner."

"He mentioned that," she recalled. And with a smile she added. "Thanks for being so honest with me, Aunt Flo." And she got up and touched her lips to the old woman's cheek.

"I'll be repaid if you avoid the mistake I made," Aunt Flo told her. "Strike or no strike, I like that Geoff Bailey!"

Grace drove home in a better frame of mind. She consulted with Hilda Olsen to make sure the evening meal would be something special. She even planned and made the dessert herself, a fancy whipped cream and tapioca mixture which Marie had always liked. Everything was arranged to make the occasion a happy one. But

211

she hadn't taken into account her father's mood.

This was unfortunate. For as soon as Adam West appeared to take his place at the head of the long table she could tell something had happened to upset him. Marie and Mike sat opposite her, behaving more like two apprehensive youngsters determined not to make any errors than anything else. It annoyed Grace that her father should inspire this fear and tension in the two newly weds rather than affection and respect.

As he finished tasting his soup, he said, "I suppose it won't be of much interest to any of you, but we've had a setback today."

Mike flashed Grace a questioning glance before he gave his attention to her father. Then he asked the older man, "Do you mean the strike was settled against the firm?"

"Not quite," Adam West said stiffly. "But we have lost some of our bargaining edge. Part of our refrigeration unit is not working properly. Unless we get the fish on hand processed and packed within twenty-four hours, it will all go bad.

And we haven't the crew to do it. The skeleton staff we're using can't possibly cope with the situation."

There was a brief moment of silence after his announcement. Then Grace said, "Wouldn't this be a sensible time to attempt arranging a settlement?"

Her father gave her a bitter smile. "I was sure you'd make that suggestion," he said. "It's what your good friend Geoff Bailey would want."

"It's what everyone in the town wants," Grace told him. "With the exception of you and your yes-men."

"I realize Dick doesn't rate as highly with you as he did," Adam West said coldly. "And I'm not looking for any help or understanding from anyone at this table."

It was Mike who surprised them all by speaking up. "I'll make you a sporting offer, Mr. West."

Her father frowned. "What do you mean?"

"You know my sympathies are with the strikers," Mike said frankly. "But it bothers me that in a world where so many are starving a quantity of food should be wasted through a stupid struggle. I'll donate my physical services as a worker in the plant until you get the fish in storage processed, on the condition you'll donate the lot of it to some needy country."

Adam West frowned. Then after a moment's deliberation, he said, "The West Packing Plant has never refused a charitable gesture. I'll take you up on that, young man."

Marie gave her husband a worried look. "I don't think you should get involved in this, Mike."

He smiled at her. "Don't worry, honey. I just want to prove to your Dad I'm not as completely useless as he thinks." And giving his attention to Adam West again, he asked, "Whom do I report to in the morning?"

"Dick Browning is heading our emergency operation," Adam West told him. "You can see him at the plant no later than seven." He seemed to take satisfaction in emphasizing the early hour.

Grace noticed that the two young people became very quiet again. And all during the meal she worried that Mike might have made a bad error. She was extremely doubtful if her father actually appreciated his unselfish gesture and she was fearful that he might somehow exploit the young man.

11

IT rained the next morning, so Grace did not go out to the Country Club for her usual game with Jamie. Instead she remained in her room writing some long-overdue letters. She'd just gotten a good start at her task when there was a light knock on the door and Marie came in. Her younger sister was wearing a pair of fawn corduroy country pants and a pale gray pullover sweater. Grace saw at once that she was on edge.

Putting down her pen, she turned to her with a smile. "Too bad it has to be so wet on your last day here," she said.

Marie nodded absently and went over to stare disconsolately out the window. Her pretty oval face with its frame of shoulder-length black hair had a pinched look that made Grace realize with astonishment how very much her sister's basic facial structure resembled Aunt Flo's. Aunt Flo must have been

216

fully as attractive as Marie when she was a girl.

Now Marie turned from her gazing at the distant elms and the garden to look at her. "I'm worried about Mike," she said with her usual directness.

"Of course you are," Grace said with understanding. "He'd have been wiser to have relaxed and spent his final day with you you."

Marie rolled her eyes in an expression of despair. "Instead he has to be the noble young man!" she said bitterly and half-turned to the window again.

"It was a fine thing he did," Grace was quick to say. "I'm sure you're proud of him."

"I'm always proud of him even when he is as stupidly naïve as this," Marie said, still looking out at the rain. "Even this day is depressing."

"You two are going to Aunt Flo's for dinner," Grace said. "I'm sure she'll have something nice for you. She'll make it an occasion."

Marie looked her way again and her face brightened some. "Aunt Flo has been marvelous to us. So different from

Dad. Why don't you come along? Let him have his dinner here alone!"

"I'm not worried about him," Grace said. "But I don't think I should join you. I'm certain Aunt Flo would like it better if she has you to herself. You know she's very fond of Mike. And she heartily approves of your marriage."

Marie looked forlorn. "It's the only encouragement we've had since we came here," she said. "Except for you, of course."

"That's why I'm glad Mike volunteered for the plant," Grace said. "Although I'm not sure he did the best thing for himself. At least he's proven to Dad he's not just a talker but someone prepared to back up his beliefs by action."

"Dad likes to make on we're all so useless," Marie said bitterly.

Grace smiled. "It's one of his weapons against us. And yet he's responsible for what we are. He insists on keeping us here under his thumb and then complains if we don't accomplish anything. At least you've defeated him. And as soon as this trouble is over I'm leaving Branton."

"Mike has asked you to come to New

York with us," she reminded her.

"Maybe I'll take him up on the offer," Grace said.

"Of course, I can't imagine Father in this place without you," Marie said.

"He'll manage. Hilda runs the household efficiently. He has Aunt Flo for company and his other friends in town."

Marie gave her a meaning glance. "Then you're breaking with Dick?"

"That's the way I feel now."

"I hope you do," Marie said with a sigh. And she crossed over and threw herself into an easy chair with her legs dangling over one of its arms. Slumped back lazily, she worried, "I don't think for a moment Dad appreciates what Mike is doing."

"I doubt it," Grace agreed.

"People of his generation are all the same," Marie complained. "Mike and I took part in a few of the protest marches in New York and one in Washington. And I know what a lot of them thought about us and the others. We're supposed to be kids not mature enough to understand how the world is run. They tell us when we're older we'll get wise and settle for things as they are."

"Do you believe that's true?"

"No," Marie said emphatically. "I'm sure it isn't. We'll go on questioning and attacking the Establishment. We have to, or the whole thing will collapse. The reform has to begin with our generation even if we don't make much headway. There isn't all that time left."

"I hope you win a bold new world," Grace said. "I'd like to be part of it. But I don't think you'll find the one we know all that easy to change."

"It means a continued battle," her younger sister agreed. "But if we don't sacrifice our beliefs to status and success like so many before us have done, we'll manage."

"I'll be interested to see Dad's reaction to Mike's going into the plant today as a laborer," Grace said.

"I noticed he didn't refuse him the privilege," her sister said. "He was hoping it was only a gesture and that Mike would back down."

"But he didn't."

"Not my Mike," Marie said proudly.

"He may be naïve, but he's not a phony."

Grace smiled. "Be thankful for that." She glanced at her watch. "The day is almost half over. He'll soon be home and you won't have to worry."

Marie sighed and managed a rueful smile of her own. "I suppose it is silly of me to go on so. But between the rain and everything else I've slipped into a mood."

"Happens to the best of us," she said. "I've been trying to catch up on some letters."

Marie got up out of the chair. "I'll let you be." She paused as she passed her. "Thanks for listening to my gripes. One of the times you really appreciate having a sister near." And with a farewell smile she went on out.

Grace was glad to see her go in a less tense mood. But she knew she wouldn't completely relax until Mike had returned from the strikebound plant. With a small sigh she began another letter.

She had no idea how long she'd been writing before she heard a car drive up in front of the house. It aroused

221

no particular interest in her until she recognized her father's voice in the hallway below. At once she dropped her pen and hurried across to the door, knowing that he hardly ever came home at noon since the strike had begun.

As she advanced downstairs she heard him asking Hilda Olsen where Marie was. The flustered housekeeper now replied to his impatient questioning with the word she thought she was upstairs having a rest. Grace passed the upset Hilda on the stairs as she went down to see her father.

Adam West was standing there with his eyes fixed on the stairs. He wore a dark raincoat and a rainhat in a matching shade. And she could tell he was badly shaken.

"What's wrong?" she asked as she reached the foot of the steps.

"I want Marie," he said arrogantly.

"What has happened?"

Her father's face was gray and for once he seemed uncertain. "There's been an accident," he said.

Her voice was harsh. "What sort of accident?"

"Someone tossed a home-made bomb into the packing section of the plant," her father admitted reluctantly. "Three of the men were injured. Mike was one of them."

"Oh, no!" she said in agonized protest. "How badly?"

"It ripped open his arm and something tore into his cheek," Adam West said. "They've taken him and the other two to the hospital. I'll drive Marie there now!"

"What's happened to Mike?" It was Marie on the stairs above them who called out the question in a hysterical voice.

"He's been injured," her father said. "Not badly I hope."

Marie came down the remaining steps and faced her father with hatred distorting her fine features. "You did it!" she cried.

"Don't be ridiculous!" Adam West retorted. "It was one of the strikers who threw that bomb!"

"You brought it on with your refusal to negotiate!" Marie sobbed. "And now Mike's had to pay for it." The girl raised her hands to cover her face and seemed about to collapse. Grace rushed to her side.

"Mike will be all right," she promised.

Adam West turned to Hilda who was hovering fearfully in the background again. "Get Marie's coat," he ordered her. "I want to drive her to the hospital."

The housekeeper brought the raincoat, and Grace helped put it on her sobbing sister. Then Adam West took over. Helping his weeping daughter to the door, he said, "It wasn't a big explosion. I'm certain Mike has no fatal injuries." He was still placating Marie as they went out in the rain to get into the car.

Grace closed the door behind them and gave the housekeeper a troubled glance. "I'm going to the hospital as well," she said. "You can take care of things here."

"Poor Miss Marie!" Hilda said, showing tears herself.

Within minutes Grace was following her father's car to the hospital. She'd decided it was better to drive there on her own rather than go with her dad and Marie in his car. This way it would give her father a chance to talk with Marie alone. They might arrive at whatever truce was possible before they reached the hospital. But she knew how Marie must feel and she didn't blame her for the rage she'd exhibited toward their father.

But there was also another side to this. Her father had explicitly stated that one of the strikers had thrown the bomb. This meant it had been a reprisal against the fire in union headquarters. And Geoff had promised her there wouldn't be any such reprisals. In a sense it was Geoff Bailey who had betrayed her trust. Geoff who had reported to the violence he'd so deplored. It made her see the handsome young union organizer in a new light.

On reaching the hospital, Grace was told that Mike had been taken to the operating room for emergency surgery. Her father and Marie were waiting together upstairs. She decided to keep her vigil in the visitor's room on the main floor. She sat alone in the medium-sized room with its view of the lobby for more than an hour before her father appeared, raincoat still on and hat in hand. His aristocratic face wore a solemn look.

Grace rose quickly. "How is he?"

"He'll be all right," Adam West said. "There will be no permanent crippling. But he'll be in bed for a while and he may need plastic surgery for his cheek."

"I see," she said in a small voice.

"Marie is remaining upstairs on the chance of being able to spend a moment or two with him," her father said. "I'm going back to the plant."

"I'll go up to her," she said.

"She's in a bad state," Adam West said worriedly. "You can drive her back to the house."

"I will."

Her father gave her a knowing look. "Now you understand the kind of people we've been dealing with. Geoff Bailey and his gangster associates have finally come out in the open."

"Please!" she begged. "I don't want to talk about it now."

"You must see that Dick and I were not wrong," her father went on. "I think even the strikers themselves will be disgusted by this lawlessness. Perhaps

226

now the farce will end."

"I see nothing farcical in Mike and those other men being hurt," Grace declared.

"You know what I mean," Adam West said. And then awkwardly, "Well, I must be on my way."

She made no reply but turned away slightly until he had gone. She had expected him to make the most of the situation. But she hadn't thought he'd bring it up so callously with Mike barely off the danger list. When she was sure he was well on his way, she started toward the lobby. It was then that she saw Geoff coming towards her.

His handsome face was strained and a frown creased his forehead. He came straight up to her. "I thought you'd be here," he said.

Grace looked at him coldly. "Well?"

"How is Mike?"

"He's going to come through it all right."

"Have you heard about the other men?"

"I don't think they're as badly injured," she said.

"Poor Marie!" he sighed. "I have no idea how this came to happen."

She gave him a derisive glance. "Isn't that asking us to be completely gullible?"

Geoff seemed startled. "Grace, you certainly don't think I was behind this madness?"

"You are leading the strikers," she told him.

"But I wouldn't condone anything of this sort," he exclaimed.

"You'll have a chance to prove that to the police's satisfaction no doubt," she said quietly.

"I'll want the police to investigate. I want to be cleared of any possible complicity in this."

"Then we can wait until that happens," she said.

He eyed her incredulously. "You're holding this against me?"

"My brother-in-law and those other men were nearly killed," she said. "What do you expect from me?"

"A little faith," Geoff said angrily.

"I think we're getting short on that," Grace told him wearily. "Please excuse me, Geoff. I have to go up to my sister."

And she walked away from him.

It was still raining heavily when she drove Marie home. The doctor gave her a strong sedative for Marie to take, and Grace saw that her near-hysterical younger sister took it as soon as they reached the house. As a result, within a half-hour Marie was sleeping soundly and the big house was cloaked in quiet.

Grace was haunted by the confrontation she'd had with Geoff. She felt she had said all the wrong things and yet she knew she could have taken no other stand. Judging by the circumstances, Geoff had to be responsible for whoever had decided to toss the home-made bomb into the plant. At the least he had failed to keep control over the men he represented. At the worst he might have encouraged the unlawful act. No matter what, he was deeply involved.

Her morbid thoughts were interrupted by the sound of a car on the gravel highway again. This time when the bell was rung impatiently she opened the door to discover a dripping Aunt Florence standing there. Wearing an old-fashioned long khaki raincoat that almost touched her toes and with a shawl of some sort over her head the old woman presented a weird appearance.

"Don't gawk at me as if I were an apparition," she snapped. "I've come to give Marie what comfort I can."

"It's good of you, Aunt Flo," she said, as the old woman came in. "But Marie is sleeping right now. The doctor gave her a sedative."

"No matter," Aunt Flo said, removing her wet scarf and glancing out the door. "I'm staying for a few days. My bags are on the way in." And, sure enough, the elderly chauffeur appeared from behind the car carrying two suitcases. When he had brought them in and deposited them in the hallway, Aunt Flo told him, "I'll call you when I want you to return for me."

"Yes, Miss West," he said and tipped his cap and went out.

After Grace closed the door behind him, her aunt said, "Now help me off with my coat and tell me all about it."

Aunt Flo's arrival proved to be a blessing. She gave Grace someone to talk to and would be there to comfort

Marie when she felt better. The old woman heard Grace's account of the unhappy events and gave a deep sigh.

"I only wish someone had thought to ask my advice," she said. "I would have certainly advised Mike against doing what he did."

"It's too late to think of that now," Grace said.

"Your father had no right to expect it of him," Aunt Flo said vehemently. "Adam has managed things badly, and I shall tell him so."

"Please don't get in a quarrel with Dad now," she begged. "Everything is confused enough as it is."

"I can handle Adam without quarreling with him," Aunt Flo told her. "I am his older sister if you'll remember."

"Father can't be blamed for this bomb business."

Aunt Flo gave her a sharp look. "You've already let Geoff Bailey know that."

"I only told him the truth."

"I can't see why you think he was directly responsible. Any one of the hundred or more strikers could have taken it into his fool head to make up that bomb and use it."

"Not if Geoff had properly warned them," she said.

"Now you're talking in theory," the old woman scoffed. "Face the facts. Geoff is probably as innocent of any wrong in this as your father. Maybe more so, since he genuinely tried to settle the strike and Adam didn't."

Grace shook her head. "I'm sorry, Aunt Flo. I can't see Geoff as all that innocent."

"You should have at least thought it over and talked to somebody else without accusing him the way you did," Aunt Flo sputtered. "It seems to me you just couldn't wait to break things up with him."

"I'm sure it's better this way," Grace said quietly.

"Well, you'll have your father's blessing in that decision, not mine," Aunt Flo said stoutly.

Marie did not want to come down for dinner. But when she woke up, Aunt Flo went to her room to talk with her. It was while the old woman was upstairs that Adam West returned for the evening bringing Dick Browning with him, Grace had not seen the young man for several days, and it struck her that he was showing the strain of the violence at the plant.

"Aunt Flo has come to stay with us a few days," she told her father before he and Dick went into the living room.

Her father's only reaction was to slightly raise his eyebrows. "Where is she now?"

"Up with Marie."

"I expect it will be good for the girl," her father said. "The trouble is Flo sometimes overdoes her kind deeds."

Dick gave Grace a thin smile. "Good to see you, honey," he said. "What's the latest word on Mike?"

"There's been no change since this morning," she said. "Marie plans to go see him this evening. I'll probably go as well."

"I doubt if they'll let you in his room until tomorrow," Adam West said in his assured way.

"I'll try anyway," she said.

Her father gave Dick a wise glance.

"Grace is beginning to understand the true nature of these union racketeers."

"The bombing sure proved that," Dick agreed at once. "I'd say in forty-eight hours the strike will be over and we'll have the men back on our own terms. And with our own union still intact."

"It looks good," her father agreed. And to her, he said, "Dick and I will be in the living room. You can call us when Flo comes down for dinner."

Grace watched the two men enter the living room with their heads together in deep conversation. She experienced a sinking sensation. There couldn't be much more real hope that Geoff Bailey would win his battle for a national union for the company.

At dinner, Aunt Flo kept Grace's father in his place. There was little he said that the old woman didn't gently chide him about. She was especially critical of his treatment of Marie and her husband.

"Mike is going to miss doing his course," she reminded him. "You must handsomely make it up to him."

Adam West frowned. "I had no way

of knowing what would happen."

"You directly sent that boy into possible danger," the old woman told him. "Don't you try to weasel out of it."

Her brother looked hurt and enraged. "I am not the kind of person who deliberately evades his responsibilities," he countered.

Aunt Flo regarded him blandly. "How fortunate, Adam. Then we needn't worry about what you'll do for those two."

In the short interim between dinner and their leaving for the hospital Dick managed to get Grace into the library for a short private conversation. The young plant manager still showed uneasiness.

"This has been a terrible day," he said. "The excitement of the explosion and then the police arriving to investigate."

"Have they made any headway?" she asked.

He shrugged. "They've brought in a captain from Bangor. He's not as free in talking as the local men."

"What sort of a bomb was it?"

"Strictly an amateur job," Dick said. "A contraption of dynamite and several flashlight batteries. The whole thing wired together. It was in a mess, but they found enough of it to get the general idea."

"If they found traces of it, shouldn't they be able to discover who made it and threw it into the plant?"

"That's what they're trying to do now," he frowned. "I doubt if they'll have any luck."

"Why not?"

Dick sighed. "For one thing, they found only pieces of the device, and then it was made up of items available without being traced."

Grace considered this. "What about fingerprints on it?"

"I don't know," he admitted.

"I hope they don't half-do the job. A lot will depend on what they find out."

Dick gave her a meaning look. "I'll bet Geoff Bailey is feeling pretty scared right now."

She hated to see the crew-cut young man enjoying Geoff's plight so. But she kept a casual tone to her reply. "It probably doesn't directly concern him."

"He must have had it tossed in there to discourage the emergency crew."

"But he's smart enough to know that endangering lives would only turn opinion against the union," she said. "Why would he want that?"

"My idea is he didn't expect the bomb to do much damage," Dick reasoned.

She frowned. "You think not?"

"No. He likely had it rigged up to throw a scare into the boys still working at the plant without intending it to do more than that. But somehow whoever made it up miscalculated, and it turned out too powerful."

"It's a possibility," she admitted.

"I'd guarantee I'm right," Dick insisted. "The way it ought to have worked no one would have been hurt, but it would have acted as a warning."

She looked up into his broad young face. "You mean like the fire?"

"The fire?"

"Yes. The one someone started at union headquarters. This was probably the strikers' way of evening the score."

"You could be right," Dick said vaguely. "Anyway I'll be glad when the strike is over. I've had to neglect you, and that hasn't been any fun."

"None of it has been any fun," she said soberly.

"I'll agree with that," he assured her. And he reached out to take her in his arms for a kiss.

"Not now," she said, pushing him away. "It's late and time we started for the hospital."

She could tell he resented her putting him off, but he said nothing. However, he was very quiet as he drove with her to the hospital. She was not anxious to talk either. She kept going over what he'd said and was surprised to find herself vaguely disturbed by the conversation. It was as if she'd missed the meaning of something he'd mentioned.

12

AT the hospital Marie was allowed to see Mike for a few minutes. She came out of his room with a smile and the news that he was making a good recovery. Grace, still troubled, had a strong desire to get away from Dick Browning to sort out her thoughts. Pleading a headache and a desire to go to bed early she dropped him off at his place. But she didn't drive directly home. Instead she headed her car toward the cottage of Dr. Ray Daniels.

The lights were on in his living room and she made her way to his front door with a feeling of relief. It was some minutes after she rang the bell before he opened the door to her.

"Sorry to keep you out there so long," he said with a smile.

"It's I who should apologize," she told him. "Coming here like this without even calling you first."

"No need to do that. I was hoping you

239

might come by soon."

She turned to face him with a sigh. "You've heard what's happened."

"I was shocked," he said, lowering himself slowly into a wing-backed chair. "How is your brother-in-law and the other men?"

"They're all doing nicely," she said.

"Thank Heavens for that," the old scholar said. "The first reports I heard hinted they might be very badly off."

"I know," she said, seating herself in an easy chair opposite him. "We were all frightened at the beginning."

"I didn't dream anything of that kind would happen."

"There were warnings," she said. "The rock that was thrown at you. And the fire in the temporary union headquarters. But those attacks were directed against the strikers."

"I've been thinking about that," he said. "I wonder if the police have come up with any suspects?"

"Not that I know of. I've only heard an account of what happened from Dick. There may be other information I haven't been told."

240

"This incident will take sympathy away from the strikers," Dr. Daniels pointed out. "I don't know what will happen now."

"I wonder," she said. "Something about Dick's version of things troubled me. But I can't seem to decide what."

"Naturally you're upset," the old man sympathized.

She gave him a direct look. "Have you seen Geoff since it happened?"

"Yes," he said. "In fact you'd have met him here if you'd gotten here an hour earlier."

"I'm glad I didn't meet him," she said, glancing down at the carpet.

"He feels very badly."

"He should."

"He's upset that you should hold him responsible," the teacher said.

"What else can I do?"

"I agree it is a complex situation," Dr. Daniels told her. "But knowing Geoff as I do I can't picture that he would encourage anything like this bomb business."

"He warned there could be reprisals against the plant."

"But he never promised anything of that sort."

She raised her eyes to meet the old man's. "But it had to be one of his men. No one else would have any reason for doing such a thing."

"Yet he mightn't be party to the act or even aware of it until after it had taken place," Dr. Daniels suggested.

"I've tried to tell myself that," she admitted. "And Aunt Flo has insisted it could have been that way. Still, I'm not convinced."

"Geoff is very discouraged about his work in Branton. And he is crushed that you've shown so little faith in him."

"Then let him come up with the guilty person and prove he had nothing to do with the bombing," Grace said.

Dr. Daniels looked glum. "I gather he is trying to do that. But he would feel differently if he knew you were on his side."

"I don't know whose side I'm on any longer. Dad tells me one thing, and Geoff says another. Each trying to prove he is in the right."

The old man gave her a weary smile.

"What advice did you get from your Aunt Flo?"

"She advised I should wait before rendering any judgement."

"It seems she's learned her lesson at last," was the veteran educator's wry comment.

"I know about you and Aunt Flo," she told him. "I've heard the whole story."

"Indeed," he said.

"I think it's wrong for you not to see each other," she argued. "You were in love and you'd have had a wonderful marriage if Aunt Flo hadn't been so anxious to please her father."

"See that you don't make the same mistake."

She looked at him guiltily. "The circumstances are so different."

"Not so different as you think," he said with a wise expression. "It will be too bad if this trouble comes between you and Geoff."

She said, "I'm just remembering."

"What?"

"The thing that's been bothering me about what Dick said. He began talking about the bomb and its construction.

243

And he said he didn't think the person who had made it intended it to be so powerful. They'd just expected to cause a diversion with it and not do any major damage."

"How could he know that?" the old man asked sharply.

She was startled. "I can't guess," she said. "Unless he was just trying to put himself in the place of the person who did the bombing."

"That doesn't seem logical," Dr. Daniels said.

She looked at the old man in shocked consternation. "Could he possibly have been in on the construction of the bomb himself?"

"From what you've told me there seems every chance of it," the old man said, sitting forward eagerly.

"But why? Why would he want to endanger the lives of the men working there or harm the plant?"

"He explained that only he put the motive down to the strikers," Dr. Daniels said triumphantly. "The bomb was thrown to give the strikers a bad name without doing any real harm. Only, as he pointed out, they miscalculated."

"Dick would never think of doing anything like that!" she protested.

"I wonder," he ruminated. "He might have some employee he could count on for his dirty work. And the same person might have made that sneak attack on me and attempted to set fire to the strikers' headquarters. It could all be the work of the same person."

"I suppose it could," she admitted.

"Do you know of anyone Dick Browning has at his beck and call? Any clever handyman who mightn't be too scrupulous?"

The name came to her with such clarity she couldn't resist saying aloud, "Joe Spear!"

"Joe Spear?" The old man frowned.

"Yes. He's a laborer at the plant. But he's very clever at electronics. And he has a strange, unpleasant sort of personality. Always seems to have a chip on his shoulder."

"Sounds the right type," Dr. Daniels said. "And he didn't join the strikers?"

"I don't think so," she said. "The other day when I went by the plant I saw him and Dick talking together."

"It all fits," Dr. Daniels said triumphantly. "I'd be willing to bet Joe Spear is our man."

She stared at him incredulously. "If that's true, Dick is involved in a criminal conspiracy!"

"That's about it," the old man said grimly. "Can't you accept it? You were quick enough to condemn Geoff Bailey."

Grace blushed. "It's just that Dick is so close to Father. And I know Dad wouldn't do such a thing."

"Your father probably knows nothing about it," the old man said. "At least I hope not for his sake. This Dick could have promoted the scheme to win the strike and prove his actions right."

"He was getting desperate," she admitted.

There was a silence in the room between them. Then the old man cleared his throat. "Well," he said quietly, "what are you going to do about it?"

"I can't do anything," she said. "All this is conjecture. We don't know for sure!"

"We never will unless we try to find out."

"But I can't go to the police with the story I've told you," she said. "They'd never take me seriously."

"I wonder," Dr. Daniels said thoughtfully. "Have you any objections to my turning this information over to a friend of mine at State Police headquarters?"

"Not if you think there is a chance of it being true."

"I say there's a strong chance or I wouldn't take action," the old man said. "We'll have to try and get the police to move in on this Joe Spear and see if they can link him to the bomb in any way."

"Whatever you think best," she said. Her head was spinning with the possibilities all this involved.

"In the meantime you mustn't say a word to anyone," the old man warned her.

"I understand," she said in a faint voice.

"It shouldn't take long to find out if we're right," Dr. Daniels said. "And I can only hope that we are."

Grace got slowly to her feet. "I just can't grasp it all at once," she said.

Dr. Daniels thrust his weight heavily on the two canes and raised himself to a standing position with his usual effort. "I don't want to rush you, my dear," he said. "But I would like to get on with this."

"Don't bother to see me to the door," she told him. "And thank you."

The old man's eyes twinkled. "Perhaps I'll have more luck in saving your romance than I did my own," he predicted.

She drove home still in a dazed state. And she was glad to find all the others had gone to bed. But getting to sleep was not easy for her. She tossed and turned as she went into all the eventualities the situation offered. And the more she went over it the more she was convinced that Dick Browning and Joe Spear might turn out to be the guilty ones. It was well on in the morning before sheer exhaustion caused her eyes to close.

The sun was shining brightly through the window of her room when she awoke. She felt weary since she'd had so little sleep and her nerves were in a jangled state. She wished she could confide in

Aunt Florence and Marie but Dr. Daniels had warned her to say nothing about the matter.

This proved more difficult than she'd expected. When she encountered Aunt Flo in the lower hallway, the imperious spinster gave her a sharp glance.

"What's come over you?"

"I don't know what you mean."

"You look positively smug," Aunt Flo told her. "Have you found out anything?"

"No, not yet," she replied, quite truthfully.

"There's something different about you this morning," the old woman insisted. And then suddenly she brightened and asked, "Have you made up with that young man?"

"Geoff Bailey?"

"Yes."

Grace shook her head. "Nothing like that."

"More's the pity," Aunt Flo told her. "I warn you, don't keep anything from me. I'll find it out eventually, and you'll be sorry."

"As soon as I hear anything I'll tell you," she promised. And she meant it.

But as yet it was a matter of waiting.

Fortunately for Grace's state of nerves the waiting didn't prove to be as long as she'd expected. The call from Dr. Daniels came in mid-afternoon. As soon as she heard the old man's excited voice on the line, she knew something must have developed in the case.

"They've pinned the bomb on your friend Joe Spear," the old man exulted. "He made a statement to the police about a half-hour ago."

"Did he implicate Dick Browning?"

"All the way. Claims Browning egged him on with it. And also put him up to that attack on me and starting the fire."

"Then they're both in serious trouble," she said. "What about Dad?"

"He seems to be in the clear. Except that he's been giving Browning too much authority. I wouldn't be surprised if the strike ended pretty fast now."

"Does Geoff know?" she asked.

"If he doesn't he soon will," the old man promised her. "If I see him do you have any message?"

"Tell him I'd like to hear from him."

"I'll be glad to do that," Dr. Daniels agreed.

"Not that I deserve to."

The old man at the other end of the line chuckled. "I don't think Geoff is one to hold grudges. Especially where a pretty girl is concerned. And by the way, I hope you'll come by this evening. I'd enjoy a half-hour's victory chat."

"I'll come by on my way back from the hospital," she said. "They're going to let us all visit with Mike for a few minutes. It will probably be close to nine."

"I'll be looking for you," he promised.

As soon as she finished on the phone, she went out to the garden where Aunt Flo and Marie were sitting. Within a few minutes she had told them all the important news.

Marie was taken aback. "I'd never have suspected Dick," she confessed.

"Neither would I have," Grace admitted. "But the way he talked bothered me. When I told Dr. Daniels, he put two and two together right away."

"Ray Daniels is a wonder," Aunt Flo said with delight. "And I never did like that young Browning." She paused. "This will really take some wind out of Adam's sails!"

"I know," Grace said. "I'm worried about Dad."

Marie was indignant. "I don't know why you should be. He hasn't been considerate of anyone else."

"Better worry about that young man you accused so unjustly," Aunt Flo said. "That Geoff fellow."

"I've been thinking about that, too," she said.

"Don't say a word to your father," Aunt Flo advised. "Just let us see how he behaves."

It was Grace who first saw her father when he returned home that afternoon. Both Marie and Aunt Flo were upstairs dressing for dinner, but she had come down early. In a way it was no accident as she'd had an idea he might be arriving sooner than usual.

Looking up from her magazine she was at once startled by the change in him. All the old arrogance was missing from his bearing and his face seemed withered and aged.

His first words were, "The strike is over."

Grace jumped up. "Wonderful! When did it happen?"

"I settled the details with young Bailey about an hour ago," her father said in a resigned tone.

"Then you did finally agree to see him," she said. "I'm glad."

His patrician face showed weariness. "There was no other choice. I feel we came to a fair compromise. The men are to have their national union affiliation and, aside from a few adjustments in working conditions, there will be no changes in their present contracts."

"That sounds good for both sides."

He nodded. "I only wish it could have come about sooner and under rather different conditions."

"Oh?" She felt he was about to reveal Dick's guilt to her.

He stood very straight. "I'm a proud man, Grace. And I like to think I'm a just one. Perhaps the disappointments in my life have made me somewhat bitter. It wasn't easy to lose your mother. And Marie has worried me. But I ask for no excuses in my behalf. I've behaved as I thought right. I've been hard when it seemed I should be. And I've made no exceptions of you or any of my family when it came to upholding my standards."

"I understand, Father," she said quietly.

He looked down and then directly at her again. "However, it seems I haven't been too discerning about my employees. I made a particularly bad error of judgement where Dick Browning was concerned." And he launched into a full explanation of Dick's part in the bombing.

When he'd finished, she said, "I'm sorry for Dick. I hope it doesn't go too badly for him."

"He knew what he was doing," Adam West said. "He almost killed my son-in-law and those other men. He must take punishment for his crime."

It was a much subdued Adam West who sat at the head of the table that evening. Grace gave her Aunt Flo credit for not twitting her brother on his complete defeat. And Marie also kept a discreet silence. Afterward they all prepared to go to the hospital. Aunt Flo voted to drive with Grace.

On the way there the old woman said, "I don't often make predictions. But I think Adam has learned his lesson at last. I doubt if he'll play the role of the heavy-handed father any more."

"It's rather pathetic," Grace said. "He seems crushed."

"Don't waste your sympathy," Aunt Flo sniffed. "He'll come around quick enough."

"It's been wonderful having you in the house," Grace said. "I wish you'd stay. I may be leaving Branton. And once Mike is well enough and he and Marie go, it will mean Dad will be alone."

"I couldn't live in the same house with him, my dear," Aunt Flo was quick to tell her. "We don't get on that well. But I'd be glad to see him for dinner two or three times a week and keep an eye on his welfare for you girls."

"That would mean a lot," Grace told her.

"Has that young man called you yet?" her aunt wanted to know.

"No."

"Too bad," Aunt Flo mourned. "You may lose him. And there aren't many young men like that who come to Branton."

"Perhaps I deserve to lose him," she said, heading the car into the hospital parking lot. "I didn't show much faith in him."

"You shouldn't be blamed," Aunt Flo said. "You've had pressure from so many people. No wonder you were confused."

"As long as the strike is settled, and Mike is going to get well."

That this was to be true became evident when they were all allowed briefly into his room. Mike propped up on pillows, looked surprisingly good. With his healthy hand he held up a telegram.

"I've finally gotten word from New York," he said. "They've arranged to have another lecturer fill in for me. But I can take over as soon as I'm well enough. I was afraid they'd cancel the whole series."

"They evidently believe you have something good to offer," Adam West said with a new appreciation for his son-in-law's abilities.

256

Marie leaned down and kissed Mike's cheek. "You're staying here until you've completely recovered," she said.

Aunt Flo tugged Grace's arm. "I think we should go and leave these young people to a few minutes' privacy," she said.

"Of course," Grace agreed.

Adam West followed them out into the corridor. "Do you want to drive back with Grace or with Marie and me?" he asked Aunt Flo.

The old woman turned to him. "I'll go with you and Marie," she said.

Grace was disappointed. She waited until her father had gone to speak with the head nurse and then she told Aunt Flo, "I hoped you'd come with me. I'm stopping at Dr. Daniels' house for a little while. I'm sure he'd like to see you."

The tall woman's thin face glowed with pleasure. "That is thoughtful of you, Grace. But not tonight. So much has happened."

"I'll tell him you were asking for him."

"Do that," Aunt Flo said brightly. "And say I'll be calling on him some day next week."

Grace smiled. "Do you really mean that?"

"Of course I do," Aunt Flo said. "After what he's done for us, I must show my appreciation." And leaning towards her confidentially, she added, "To tell the truth, I've been looking for a good excuse to see him for a long time."

So Grace drove away from the hospital with a mild feeling of elation. At least she had some good news for Dr. Daniels. And he certainly deserved it. Not only had he been her friend all along, but he had been instrumental in clearing up the mess at the plant.

The only thing he hadn't managed was to repair the difference between herself and Geoff. But she could hardly expect that of him after he'd done so much else for them. And it had been her own lack of faith in Geoff that had been responsible.

Dusk was settling as she parked her car in front of the cottage, but the living room windows showed a cheery light. She walked up the path and was going to ring the bell when she saw the door had been left ajar.

She stepped inside and went down the hall and into the living room to find Geoff Bailey standing there. The handsome young man smiled. "Surprised?"

"A little," she confessed.

"Dr. Daniels is waiting for us in the library," he said. "But I wanted to say hello first."

"Hello," she said softly.

"There'll never be another goodbye," he promised her as he took her in his arms for the kiss she'd been waiting for. She relaxed in the security of his embrace. Content, she had at last found her true love.

THE END

THE WILDERNESS WALK
Sheila Bishop

Stifling unpleasant memories of a misbegotten romance in Cleave with Lord Francis Aubrey, Lavinia goes on holiday there with her sister. The two women are thrust into a romantic intrigue involving none other than Lord Francis.

THE RELUCTANT GUEST
Rosalind Brett

Ann Calvert went to spend a month on a South African farm with Theo Borland and his sister. They both proved to be different from her first idea of them, and there was Storr Peterson — the most disturbing man she had ever met.

ONE ENCHANTED SUMMER
Anne Tedlock Brooks

A tale of mystery and romance and a girl who found both during one enchanted summer.

CLOUD OVER MALVERTON
Nancy Buckingham

Dulcie soon realises that something is seriously wrong at Malverton, and when violence strikes she is horrified to find herself under suspicion of murder.

AFTER THOUGHTS
Max Bygraves

The Cockney entertainer tells stories of his East End childhood, of his RAF days, and his post-war showbusiness successes and friendships with fellow comedians.

MOONLIGHT
AND MARCH ROSES
D. Y. Cameron

Lynn's search to trace a missing girl takes her to Spain, where she meets Clive Hendon. While untangling the situation, she untangles her emotions and decides on her own future.

NURSE ALICE IN LOVE
Theresa Charles

Accepting the post of nurse to little Fernie Sherrod, Alice Everton could not guess at the romance, suspense and danger which lay ahead at the Sherrod's isolated estate.

POIROT INVESTIGATES
Agatha Christie

Two things bind these eleven stories together — the brilliance and uncanny skill of the diminutive Belgian detective, and the stupidity of his Watson-like partner, Captain Hastings.

LET LOOSE THE TIGERS
Josephine Cox

Queenie promised to find the long-lost son of the frail, elderly murderess, Hannah Jason. But her enquiries threatened to unlock the cage where crucial secrets had long been held captive.

THE TWILIGHT MAN
Frank Gruber

Jim Rand lives alone in the California desert awaiting death. Into his hermit existence comes a teenage girl who blows both his past and his brief future wide open.

DOG IN THE DARK
Gerald Hammond

Jim Cunningham breeds and trains gun dogs, and his antagonism towards the devotees of show spaniels earns him many enemies. So when one of them is found murdered, the police are on his doorstep within hours.

THE RED KNIGHT
Geoffrey Moxon

When he finds himself a pawn on the chessboard of international espionage with his family in constant danger, Guy Trent becomes embroiled in moves and countermoves which may mean life or death for Western scientists.

TIGER TIGER
Frank Ryan

A young man involved in drugs is found murdered. This is the first event which will draw Detective Inspector Sandy Woodings into a whirlpool of murder and deceit.

CAROLINE MINUSCULE
Andrew Taylor

Caroline Minuscule, a medieval script, is the first clue to the whereabouts of a cache of diamonds. The search becomes a deadly kind of fairy story in which several murders have an other-worldly quality.

LONG CHAIN OF DEATH
Sarah Wolf

During the Second World War four American teenagers from the same town join the Army together. Forty-two years later, the son of one of the soldiers realises that someone is systematically wiping out the families of the four men.

THE LISTERDALE MYSTERY
Agatha Christie

Twelve short stories ranging from the light-hearted to the macabre, diverse mysteries ingeniously and plausibly contrived and convincingly unravelled.

TO BE LOVED
Lynne Collins

Andrew married the woman he had always loved despite the knowledge that Sarah married him for reasons of her own. So much heartache could have been avoided if only he had known how vital it was to be loved.

ACCUSED NURSE
Jane Converse

Paula found herself accused of a crime which could cost her her job, her nurse's reputation, and even the man she loved, unless the truth came to light.